Advance Praise for *Sin in The Big Easy*

"A fresh take on the New Orleans legal thriller, Elizabeth McCourt's *Sin in The Big Easy* also introduces a fresh take on the lawyer-hero, Abby Callahan. We can't help but like Abby, an engagingly messy character, trying to bring some order to a messy life, including a messy family and a messy romantic history. Abby is conspicuously good-hearted, charmingly uninhibited about sex, but she also drinks too much and seems as capable as any of us of repeatedly misjudging the world and the characters who inhabit it. McCourt gets the legal proceedings off to a good start, with a diminished-capacity rape case, a mysterious victim, and a suitably privileged defendant. In the first of many twists, as the case begins the judge is suddenly arrested and escorted out of his own courtroom. From that point forward, appropriately, nothing is ever what it seems. Who knows what exotic locale Elizabeth McCourt will choose for Abby's next adventure, but I'm sure her fans will follow her anywhere."

— Robert Reeves, Publisher, *The Southampton Review*

"Abby Callahan is just the kind of super investigator D.A. we need— smart, athletic, and daring. Intricately plotted, *Sin in The Big Easy* will keep readers guessing as to who can and cannot be trusted until the very last page. With her debut novel Elizabeth McCourt has created such a compelling legal thriller—the stakes are high. Very high."

— Lou Ann Walker, Author, *A Loss for Words*

"I was immediately drawn to this first in a new series by Elizabeth McCourt, the creator of a sharp, smart, yet complicated assistant D.A. Abby Callahan, who, on her morning run, discovers a bloodied victim of sexual abuse. The girl's vulnerability is a perfect match for Abby's pride and ambition to seek justice, but McCourt cleverly invents deeply emotional roadblocks that will surprise and keep you wanting more."

— Sande Boritz Berger, Author, *The Sweetness*

SIN IN THE BIG EASY

VOLUME 1
ABBY CALLAHAN MYSTERIES

ELIZABETH MCCOURT

A POST HILL PRESS BOOK
ISBN: 978-1-68261-576-8
ISBN (eBook): 978-1-68261-577-5

Sin in The Big Easy
© 2018 by Elizabeth McCourt
All Rights Reserved

Cover art by Christian Bentulan

Post Hill Press
New York • Nashville
posthillpress.com

Published in the United States of America

*This book is dedicated to Mary, Marci, and Frankie,
who each encouraged and inspired me to be fearless.*

CHAPTER 1
New Orleans, Louisiana

•••■•———————•———————•■•••

As soon as I stepped out of my apartment on St. Mary's Street, I felt the air stick to my skin. I pulled my hair back into a ponytail, adjusted my hat's visor, and headed up to the streetcar tracks, about a block away. I jogged on the tracks, ready for an oncoming car, relishing the warm breeze as another streetcar rumbled by in the opposite direction, clanging its bell as it passed. The grass in the middle of the track was worn down but hard-packed, which was better than running on the uneven pavement, damaged by the last few storms, and dodging people and cars. St. Charles Avenue was waking up with people walking dogs, parents driving kids around, and others headed home from the bars or going to work. For the first time in weeks, I didn't have to be in court until nine, so I had time to run all the way up to Audubon Park. Since law school, the park was my favorite place to run, not only for its evenly paved track, but for the beauty of every section and the shaded areas on sunny days.

I passed the statue in the front of the Loyola campus that everyone calls Touchdown Jesus, which always made me think of my parents. Crossing the street heading into the park, I looked at my watch and started around the track. I felt the droplets of sweat under my chest dripping down onto my stomach. I wiped my brow with my hand and adjusted my visor. As I turned a bend in the track, I passed a few people but not anyone I recognized. I accelerated to the shade of one of the massive live oak trees, its moss-laden branches cresting over the track, then slowed and timed myself for thirty seconds before accelerating again. My old criminal law professor, who did a lot of 5K races and often saw me in the park, had told me I needed to speed up a little bit if I ever wanted to get faster. He was the one who encouraged me to intern at the DA's office during law school. I don't think even he could have predicted that I would have turned it into my default career. I'd applied to some of the big firms and gotten a few interviews, but mostly I received polite rejection letters. I repeated my thirty seconds of speeding up and thirty seconds of rest method, sprinting around the park's track. I was panting hard when I rounded the bend coming back to where I'd started. I veered off the track, my sneakers crunching on the gravel, and I slowed to a walk heading towards the playground area to hit the drinking fountain over by the swings. The swings were moving from the tiniest breeze, but otherwise all was quiet.

The water in the fountain was warm, and I let it cascade over the side of the bowl for a minute. I tested it with my hand, then leaned down and slurped some of the metallic-tasting, still-warm water. I closed my eyes and let the water splash into my face, shaking it off like a dog and wiping my eyes with my shirt.

"Over here, please help me!" A woman's voice yelped through sobs.

I spun around and saw a woman lying on the dirt at the base of a big oak tree. I hadn't noticed her before.

"Please, over here," the women's words slurred.

"Are you okay? Shit! What happened?" I jogged over and knelt beside her. She looked like she was about twenty, with her long curly hair half out of her ponytail, her face smudged with dirt. She was wearing a short skirt and a shimmering gold-and-black top; clearly, she'd been out the night before and never gone home. She tried to hide a pair of bloodied underwear clutched in her left hand. As I moved closer, I saw a bump on her forehead that had broken the skin. "Don't move, I'll go and get you some help."

"Please don't leave me," she said as her voice cracked. She shuddered, then grabbed the tree and tried to get up, but her knees buckled and she stepped back.

"You're okay now. Do you have your purse? Your phone?" I'd decided to go without anything except my house key and my watch this morning.

"I must have dropped it when I was running from him and then I tripped and must have passed out. I found these lying over there," she said, pointing towards the back of the playground area and then looking down at the underwear. She started to sob and when she put her hand up to her forehead, she winced.

"Should I take another look over there for your purse?" I asked as I tried to console her.

"You can check, if you want to," she said, letting her tears fall down her cheeks.

I ran over to where she had pointed and scanned the ground, but not wanting to leave her alone, I ran back. I crouched down next to her and held out my hand and said, "Do you think maybe you dropped it somewhere else? Let me walk you over to the fountain to get some water, then I'll get help…." She looked at her bloodied underwear and started to cry again.

I grabbed her hand and squeezed. "Come on, let's get you up and out of here."

"Thank you for not running away. Someone else was here earlier and I thought she was going to help, but then she went away." I could smell the alcohol still on her breath when she said this. She took my hand, stood up and wobbled. "I'm okay, I've got it." She steadied herself, gripping my elbow.

"Hang on to me and we'll walk slowly." I held her as she fumbled and fixed her skirt, hiding the scratches and bruising on her inner thigh, pressing it with her hands as if she were trying to get the wrinkles out.

"I feel like an idiot," she said and wiped her face. "I'm Darcy."

"You're not an idiot and you're going to be okay, Darcy. I'm Abby." I led her across the jungle gym area, and she stopped again to pull down her skirt. She hunched her shoulders, held her hand to her chest, and tried to cover her skin with her ripped shirt. We crossed a grassy area without trees. The sun beat down on us, and I pulled my visor down on my head and saw sweat beading on Darcy's brow. More cars were flowing on St. Charles and people were starting to enter the park.

"I'm fine now," Darcy said and gently pushed away from me. "Maybe you can just help me get home." Her flat accent had Midwestern tones.

"Sure, we can do that, but I really think you should get yourself looked at by a doctor just in case you're hurt more than you think." I knew what could happen. I'd been afraid to go to the hospital, too, and since I didn't, I was never able to press charges.

"I think if I just go home and clean up, I'll feel better. People are staring at me." I looked around and saw one elderly man walking with a yapping black Westie, who scowled and turned the other way.

"Listen, I know what you're going through. I've been there. You need to get yourself checked out, especially if you were knocked out. You need to make sure you don't have a concussion."

"I don't want to get anyone in trouble!"

"You won't get in trouble. You didn't do anything wrong." I nearly bellowed when I said this. I wanted to shake her and tell her it wasn't her fault, she didn't ask for it, that people would believe her and that she didn't have to be afraid of what people were going to think. I knew how alone she was feeling.

"The guy who I was with, he…" Darcy's lower lip quivered.

"He can't hurt you now, Darcy. I'm going to help you make sure of that. Walk with me over to the sidewalk and we'll find a phone, or we can hop on the streetcar and go straight to the hospital." She gripped my arm so hard I thought I was going to bruise.

"Abby, you've been so nice to me. Thank you." Her face softened and she started to tear again.

I squeezed her hand gently and continued toward the sidewalk and scanned for someone with a phone. Darcy started walking slower and limping.

"Let's stop for a second and take a few breaths," I said. As we got closer to St. Charles, I saw a woman with a baby carriage and knew she'd have a phone. Darcy looked down at the ground, away from me, but I could see her tears rolling down her face. She was breathing hard, as if she'd been the one running.

"Can I please use your phone?" The woman looked at us wide-eyed and dug into her bag, handing me her phone. While rocking the baby, she pulled out some wipes and handed them to Darcy. "Thank you so much," I said and called the ambulance.

"Are you sure I'll be okay if I go to the hospital? I don't want to make a scene," Darcy whispered to me as the police and ambulance arrived and started taking out the stretcher.

"It won't take long and I'll go with you, okay?" Someone could cover my cases for an hour or so; I'd need to call the office and see who was available.

"If you must be somewhere, Abby, you should go," Darcy said as they were putting her into the ambulance.

"Darcy, I'm going to get the guy who did this to you if you let me help you."

"You coming?" A big paramedic, with fingers thick like sausage, put his hand out for me to climb into the rig.

"Just wait one second," I said. I told the police officers where I found her so that they could take a quick look around to see if they might find anything. The one cop rolled his eyes at me until I told him that I worked at the DA's office.

"Alright, Miss, for you, we'll give it a quick look," he said and headed off in the direction of the swings.

"I'm ready to go," I said and stepped up into the ambulance, sitting down on the bench against the window. Darcy was in the stretcher in the middle covered by a light sheet and belted in except for her arms. Sprinkles of blood speckled the lower part of the sheet. The paramedic snapped an ice pack, put it in a cloth, and laid it on Darcy's head, placing her hand on top of it to hold it in place. He wrapped a blood pressure cuff around her arm and pulled a stethoscope out of a cubby over her head.

"Don't be scared, Darcy," I said.

She looked at me and reached out and dropped the ice pack. I picked it up and grabbed her hand. The siren of the ambulance screeched as we ran through the red lights all the way down St. Charles, but it felt like we were in a tunnel. I was surprised to see how much equipment was stuffed in every little cubby in the back of the rig. Darcy shut her eyes. The paramedic scribbled notes on his clipboard and the driver spoke code on the radio to the hospital.

The paramedic wrote a few notes after taking the cuff off her arm and asked, "Are you hurt anywhere else?" Darcy put her other hand on her stomach and tried to turn over, but the belts were too tight. He loosened them. "I think I have what I need. You're going to be alright," he said and looked over at me with his eyebrows raised. I started to agree, but when I opened my mouth I had nothing to say.

CHAPTER 2

Two months later

I was already sweating through my white blouse under my blue suit—the air-conditioning was always broken in our office. I'd practiced my opening statement so many times, I was confident it would go off without a hitch, but Darcy was late. I'd fibbed to Darcy about court starting at nine so we'd have a chance at being on time for Judge Kehoe. My heart was pounding. I sucked down the last of my iced coffee and tried to relax. I wanted to prove everyone wrong—this rape case could be won. Pacing by the window of my shoebox-sized office, which I shared with another newbie ADA, I hoped that the jury would be able to see what I'd seen that morning a few months ago in Audubon Park.

I walked around to my faux-wood desk that abutted my office mate's and pretended to be busy. While waiting for my computer to boot up so I could review a few more notes or at least check my email, I sifted through my desk drawer. There were the five postcards from Val, who was already three weeks into our six-month trip around the world that I'd opted not to go on because I had gotten this job in the DA's office.

* * *

"Blow it off, Abby," Val said when I told her that I just couldn't follow through on my promise to take the trip we'd been planning for years. "It's a job, you'll get another one. What's the big deal?" Val, my best and longest friend from kindergarten, had been living a week-to-week life waitressing in New York to Florida and back since we'd graduated from high school. She worked and then traveled in her offseason, always begging me to go with her. I'd tried to meet up with her when I could, once when she was waitressing in St. Thomas and another time when she was traveling with a surfer boyfriend in Puerto Escondido, Mexico. Even before law school, we'd been planning the trip around the world.

"It's not that simple, Val. I have this degree and a huge student loan. I need to get a real job, and then I can take a break." She didn't talk to me for a few weeks and then called me the day before she was leaving to say goodbye.

Almost every day I looked at Val's postcards and emails. In Oahu, she'd run up Diamond Head. She met some surfers in Kauai and managed to exchange beer for surfing lessons in Hanalei Bay. On the giant Sleeping Buddha postcard from Bangkok, she told me about watching bootlegged movies and eating Pad Thai on Kho San Road. She was headed to islands where, she told me, she'd be eating green curry shrimp every day while getting scuba-certified. She'd even sent a postcard from her stopover in Alaska.

* * *

"Look, I'm on time, I'm on time!" Darcy flew into my office and tossed her red messenger bag full of books on the ground. When she swung around to look at the clock above the door, she knocked over the stack of files I had arranged precariously on the left corner of my desk.

"We need to leave now…." I bent down to pick up the files and tried to compose myself without blasting her. "You look nice." Darcy squirmed when I said this, running her fingers through her hair. She was a bit sweaty and in disarray from running but aside from her chipped red nail polish, she wore an almost respectable-length black skirt and high-heeled black sandals. I took a deep breath.

When my phone rang, I answered, thinking it might be related to the case. "Abigail Callahan." I answered.

"Abby?" my mother said. She sounded early-evening drunk. Although it was tempting to hang up, I knew it would be better to appease her or she wouldn't stop calling for the rest of the morning.

"Got to make it quick, Ma, I'm on my way over to the trial." Standing, I gathered the necessary files, shoved them in my briefcase, and motioned to Darcy to speed things up.

"Your father needs to see you; he's not doing that great. He needs to see you." She started to get choked up.

"I know, Ma, I know. Listen, I'll call you when I get a break later this afternoon, and we can talk some more about this. I'm sorry, but right now I have to go, I can't be late for this judge."

"Good luck then, Abigail," she said and hung up. After Dad's diagnosis, I'd been meaning to get home, but I hadn't felt pressed to do it. He seemed to be managing with the chemo and the prognosis seemed positive.

"Do you have it together, Darce? Know what you have to do in there?" I pulled my long brown ponytail, feeling guilty about last week when I harped on Darcy about her clothes. When I said that I didn't want the jury to perceive her as a bimbo, she started to cry, which made me feel terrible. I'd only wanted her to be aware of what we were up against so she'd be prepared.

Everyone, including my friend, Jill, and my boss, had been trying to talk me out of going forward with this case. "You can't win it. You just feel responsible because you found her and you want to help." Maybe they were right, but that couldn't sway my determination. Since I hadn't gone on that trip with Val, I was surely going to try to do something good with my career.

Darcy pulled her skirt down against her tanned thighs. If I noticed her legs, I wondered what the judge would think. Maybe the jury wouldn't pay attention when she walked over to the jury stand. Unlikely. But it was too late now and we needed to head over to court.

"Abby, I'm nervous and want to get this over with," she said as we got into the elevator taking us down to the garage.

Me too, I thought, but said, "You're going to do great."

"Your dad doing any better?" her tone reminded me of the old Darcy I met at the hospital a few weeks ago when we started this case.

"It doesn't look good. He's just getting worse and worse. After we win, I'm headed up to New York for a visit. The chemo is absolutely killing him."

My mother had been calling so much lately that it was hard for anyone not to notice. In a way, Darcy knowing part of my story was good. I think it made her trust me. While I was visiting her at the hospital, we talked a lot.

"Chip didn't pressure me the first time we had sex, but after that it was just weird working at the same place, so I didn't want to anymore," she disclosed to me one afternoon, which I knew would confuse things. After the ambulance trip from Audubon Park, she stayed at the hospital for a few days because of internal bleeding and a possible concussion. I visited her every day.

"Just because you gave someone consent once doesn't give them the right to take it again," I told her. I knew that wasn't going to help our case, but I hoped that a smart jury would still sympathize with her.

"Everyone at school liked him. He'd come around the sorority house, just to visit me, and then he'd talk to my friends."

I didn't believe that he was just some sweet guy coming by a sorority house to say hello, but I let her continue.

"Me and Chip were having drinks that night and I must have had a lot because the last thing I remembered was being at the club drinking this crazy drink, what was it called—which tasted like Kool-Aid by the way. When I woke up, he was making me breakfast and kissing me. I was afraid to tell him that I didn't remember, and he seemed so sweet."

I knew that Darcy was afraid that she was going to be perceived as a slut, but she was even more afraid of Chip and his dad's connections. Ever since we'd refused to drop the charges against him, she'd gotten more hang-ups on her phone than usual and often had the feeling she was being followed. We'd gotten into the parking garage and hurried over to my old navy-blue Honda Accord. I clicked the lock open and we both got in, throwing her bag and my briefcase in the back seat.

"Let's do a little more prep on the way over." I glanced into the rearview mirror to make sure my mascara hadn't smudged. I only wore makeup on court days.

"I drank, he wouldn't take me home, and then he fucked me and left me for dead in the park. No one is going to believe me." Darcy looked out the window and rubbed her eyes, then started fiddling with the radio that was already playing some mellow jazz on WOOZ.

"Darcy, we're almost there, and I know you can do this. They are going to believe you. Please, I want us to focus and get there on time so we can do a great job." I didn't want to show how nervous I was; I did *believe* in this case. Chip needed to be taught a lesson that his dad couldn't bail him out every time he violated another woman. Although I couldn't find any documented proof, my guess is that this wasn't the first time that Chip had gotten himself in a situation like this. It was probably the first time that someone called him on it and his daddy couldn't clean up the mess.

"What if he comes after me, Abby?" Darcy's tone was soft, like a little girl's.

"That's exactly why we're doing this. You're strong, Darcy, and you have me. We've got to stop him from doing this to someone else."

"Abby, I'm scared."

"Darcy, you're braver than I was. Don't be like me; you'll regret it your whole life."

"You think so?" She shifted in her seat, pushed her hair back and I believed, once again, that she was an innocent twenty-year-old who'd just gotten caught up with the wrong guy.

"I'm on your side, and I won't let you down. I promise," I said. Guys like Chip made me so angry and if we could stop him from doing this to someone else I think we could both feel great.

"Any final words?"

"Tell the truth and answer my questions. Most important, don't elaborate for the defense, just answer 'Yes' or 'No,' if possible. The defense attorney will try to distract you; just slow down and look at me if you get nervous."

I was worried about Elias, the defense attorney. He had a way of making witnesses, especially ones like Darcy, scramble their words and turn them around. The other problem was, not only was Elias smart, but he had the most outrageous lazy eye that was completely distracting to witnesses. Between his good ol' boy style and the lazy eye, he could get witnesses into a trance. Luckily, I'd had quite a few misdemeanor cases against him and had even won a few, but sometimes witnesses couldn't get past that eye.

At twenty-five after nine, we arrived at the courthouse and hustled up the steps. "Morning, Abby," said Darren as I flashed my ID badge.

"How's it going, Darren?" I said as I waved Darcy in through the metal detector. He ogled her and winked at me.

"Knock 'em dead, kid," he said. I nodded with a smile, even though I wanted to give him the finger, and headed to the right with Darcy in tow.

We found our way to Judge Kehoe's courtroom, a sea of blue suits with black briefcases. Darcy winced and cleared her throat. I told her to sit while I went up to the clerk to check in.

Elias and Chip were in the second row and looked like they were old friends at a party. Chip had a new haircut and wore an expensive pinstriped blue suit he had probably borrowed from his father. He looked like any fraternity boy dressed up for a formal. I gave Elias a nod. Chip looked back at Darcy and smirked. Darcy stayed stoic and didn't acknowledge him. I hoped we would get through our opening statements before noon.

We waited while the court went through a short docket of mostly pleas and continuances that took about an hour. I couldn't blame the judge for not wanting to be backlogged after a two-day trial. He ordered a short recess and the sea of suits started to dissipate. Darcy started to fidget. She whispered to me that she was going to go to the bathroom, and just then, the clerk called out, "The State of Louisiana versus Richard Hebert Junior." The clerk went to the back room to gather up the jury while I moved Darcy and myself beyond the gate into the corral of the immediate courtroom.

We sat down at the large oak table to the left side of the room, away from the jury. Chip and Elias sat right next to the jury box, as we had agreed during motion hearings last week. I pulled out two yellow legal pads from my briefcase and gave one to Darcy and whispered, "Write down any questions or if you remember something you forgot to tell me. I'm assuming I know everything, right?" Darcy looked at me wide-eyed, then nodded.

"Is the State ready to proceed?" Judge Kehoe directed in his monotone drawl, which somehow made him sound like he was from Brooklyn. The judge had been a defense attorney in his prior life and didn't have a lot of patience for the DA's office.

"We are, Your Honor." I stood up.

"Defense?" he asked.

"We are as well, Your Honor," said Elias, who stood and sat down again.

"Ms. Callahan, you may begin," said the judge and he rocked back on his chair like he might be considering a nap.

"Thank you, Your Honor." I strategically stood next to Darcy for the first part of the opening.

"May it please the court, ladies and gentlemen of the jury," I said and began by telling Darcy's story.

CHAPTER 3

"**A**nd the evidence will show that the defendant and Darcy left F&M's together," I said as I stood in front of the jury. I concentrated on making sure my hand motions were meaningful. After watching myself on video during my advanced evidence class in law school, I knew I could look like an idiot with hands moving all over the place, as if I were at a cocktail party chatting with my girlfriends or a patient in an insane asylum.

I told them about how Darcy had been drinking and passed out in the car on the ride over to the park. "When they got to the park, Darcy came to, and only agreed to get out and walk if Chip would take her home right afterwards.

"Darcy and Chip had one prior consensual sexual encounter," I said. A female member of the jury shifted in her seat and diverted her eyes to the floor. "You will see photographs of her bruises and scrapes from the incident and from the trauma of being in the park overnight." I told the jury what they would hear from the medical testimony and evidence from her clothing. I didn't want to box myself in by saying that Darcy would testify. I still wanted to keep that option open in case I decided that we could win without her testimony.

The worst thing that could happen would be Darcy taking the stand, then falling into a rhythm of "Yes" or "No" questions from

Elias from which I couldn't protect her. I was afraid that she would admit feeling confused and jilted by Chip, which would give the jury reasonable doubt about the validity of the rape. I'd gotten the testimony knocked out about Darcy being blackballed from her sorority because of Chip's sister, but Darcy was nervous, and Elias would look to exploit that.

"As jurors, I thank you and urge you to pay close attention to the evidence and details so that you will come to a decision where justice will be...served," I'd finished despite the door slamming at the back of the courtroom, and when I'd glanced back I saw two police officers walking in. I shrugged it off. There was a lot of interest in this case because not only did it get a spot in *The Times-Picayune*, but *The Gambit* had run a story on date rape, mentioning the DA's office and lack of police cooperation on this case, inferring it was probably because of Chip's dad, according to a source. I walked back to my seat and tried hard not to flop down with relief. The air in the confining courtroom was starting to smell like the French Quarter on a hot day. The judge waved his hand and whispered something to the court clerk.

When I'd started working with Darcy, I hadn't realized how connected Chip was, even though I knew that his father was a well-known defense lawyer. My boss, Bruce, who was also my supervising attorney, gave me the scoop on Chip when I told him I wasn't going to plea out the case. He said a friend of his over in the NOPD told him that things had a way of disappearing when it came to Chip Hebert. Unfortunately, nothing Bruce found out could be admitted, and he didn't really have any factual details, only that there was some assault stuff and a few college fraternity fights involving alcohol. With no real evidence or paper trail, I had a boatload of hearsay, but not much else.

"We are going to take a fifteen-minute recess, and then will continue with opening statements," the judge said.

The clerk shuffled the jury into the side room and then went to the back of the room towards the officers, inviting them into the judge's chambers. I looked at Elias, who was looking ahead, writing notes for his opening statement. Chip looked over at the cops and looked away, then back again to the rear of the courtroom.

I looked back at the cops, then at Chip, and over to the judge, who was waving his hands, giving instructions to his clerk. If the case was continued, I wasn't sure if I could convince Bruce to let me keep moving forward. I gestured to Darcy to come with me outside the courtroom during the recess.

"What's with those cops who went into the judge's chambers?" she asked. We both walked into the bathroom to freshen up. She put her bag on top of the sink and started digging for more makeup while I went into a stall.

"I'm sure it has to do with another case or maybe they need a warrant signed by the judge that can't wait." I didn't want to admit to Darcy that I was concerned.

"Is this going to be over soon?" She sounded exasperated.

"Darcy, just look forward and write notes when you get nervous. We'll probably break for lunch before anything else happens." I washed my hands and used the paper towel to wipe off some of the mascara that had melted under my eyes. Other than that, I looked pulled together, lawyerly even. My father would be proud. "Let's get back in there and show Chip that you are not afraid." I squeezed her shoulder. I thought, we can win this, I know we can.

When we got back into the courtroom the cops were flanking the judge. He was talking loudly, "You don't have anything! How dare you interrupt my courtroom! I'll sue you myself!" Darcy and I stood at the back of the courtroom until it finally looked like the judge agreed to walk out. They cuffed him and took him out the side door. I walked up to Elias.

"It's only been five minutes. What the hell happened?" I barked.

"Looks like we're continued," Elias said and started putting his files back into his briefcase, cleaning up his table.

"This is ridiculous—Elias…" I was tempted to say something about Elias having something to do with this but thought better of it.

Elias picked up his briefcase, signaling to Chip to follow. "All I know is, at this point, you should be expecting a motion to dismiss. You don't have a chance…" he said to me.

For a moment, I was enraptured by his lazy eye. "I look forward to that," I lied. If he didn't get his motion to dismiss, surely Darcy would lose her steam or Bruce would force my hand.

"I was looking forward to this. Until next time." Elias smirked. "Abby, you sure you don't want to start working for the dark side?"

"Not a chance, Elias."

Elias winked at me and walked away as Darcy was coming up to me from the other side of the courtroom.

"What's going on?" Darcy said.

"Well, we are continued until we are assigned a new judge."

"Must have been Chip's dad—I knew something like this was going to happen!"

My mind was churning. "I'm sure it's something bizarre that has nothing to do with you. Just go home now, and I'll call you as soon as I know more." Although it was possible that she was right, I needed to find out before I started speculating what happened in the judge's chambers. With this glitch, Bruce might tell me to drop it and then gloat that it was a waste of time.

"If we're not going to do this today, then I'm finished. I want this to be over." Darcy was already dialing her cellphone.

I gathered my notepads and shoved them into my briefcase. "Darcy, check in with me later today to see if we know anything."

"I'm scared, Abby."

"Darcy, we're going to see this through, trust me, okay? You're going to be okay and we're going to work this out." She nodded, gave me a hug, and left the room.

If another judge didn't take this case right away, Elias would be able to argue right to a speedy trial and probably win on that technicality, but I was going to do everything possible to prevent that. I had to head back and get working on my response to Elias's motion.

I headed out of the courthouse and Darren yelled, "Have a nice day, young lady!"

"Catch you next time, Darren," I said.

I stepped outside and turned on my phone. "Jesus, ten calls!" It was hazy, and I put on my big French Market sunglasses. I pressed redial and was relieved when it hit the third ring. I could tell Mom was completely panicked but maybe things had died down.

"Abby, where have you been, where have you been?" Mom said this so quickly I had a hard time understanding her.

"Remember, I was in trial. I'm on break. You've sent me a million messages. What's going on?"

"It's your father. He's...he's missing. No one can find him!" she said. I was confused that she hadn't mentioned this to me earlier.

"Did you call the firehouse? Charlie? What about the hardware store?"

"You know he's been going around giving people goodbye letters." She started to cry.

"It doesn't mean anything." Mom was forgetful and this wasn't the first time this had happened, especially when she was drinking. One time, she'd called the police, only to remember after two hours that Dad had gone fishing with Charlie out in Montauk for the day.

"What if he...what if he actually did something?" she whimpered.

"Call Bill at the police station, have a few of the guys look for him. Then call me back and let me know what happened." Then I thought better of it and said, "You sit down, make some coffee. I will call Bill, someone will call me, then I will call you."

Instead of taking out an APB, I figured it would be good to give Jason, my ex-boyfriend, a call to push things along. We were still friendly even after I'd broken off the relationship and gone to law school. He'd stopped hating me after he'd gotten laid again, which he'd called to tell me about the next day and then told me, "I'm so over you."

"Jason, hey, it's Abby," I said stoically.

"What's up?" Jason was just as abrupt.

"I'm sorry to bother you, but Dad is missing, and I thought you might be able to help. Would you mind checking around?"

"No problem," he said and hung up. My dad had been Jason's baseball coach when he was a kid. When we'd broken up, my dad might have been more disappointed than me.

I got back to the office, sat down, and immediately started going through the files stacked on my desk. Then, I turned to my computer to start my response for Elias's motion. I already knew exactly what he was going to say. All I wanted was a dismissal without prejudice so I could refile. This fiasco with the judge and the case could potentially set me back months in misdemeanors, but I wasn't about to give up on Darcy.

I picked up my office phone on the first ring and hoped it was Jason, "Hey, Abby, want to meet me for happy hour? I just heard what happened."

"Uh, hey, Jill, how'd you hear so fast?" Jill was probably my best friend and since she worked at *The Times-Picayune* as a freelancer, she always seemed to know gossip at lightning speed.

"You know, I have my sources. Actually, I knew you were there so I thought I'd try to see some of the trial today along with some other stuff I was covering at the courthouse."

"Can you ask your dad if he's heard anything really bad about

Judge Kehoe that might explain why he got nearly dragged out of the courtroom by the police?" Jill's dad was a prominent New Orleans attorney himself, although he mostly focused on maritime issues. Jill also worked part-time for him because the pay at the paper was a pittance, but Jill was convinced she needed to cut her teeth there so she could be a traveling journalist on assignment.

"Listen, let's meet for happy hour. Call me when you get off and I'll meet you," she said and hung up.

"Hey there, Abby," said Bruce, popping his head in my door.

"You heard?"

"Seeing you back here this early isn't a good sign. What happened?"

"Judge got thrown out, busted by the police or something." I put my hand to my temple and pressed hard as if to massage the headache that was not there yet.

"You got your bullet points yet for your response to the motion to dismiss?"

"I'm working on that now," I said.

"Well, finish it up—not like it's going to get filed today. First thing Monday morning, let me read over it, and then you can file it by noon once you review the motion. We're headed over to Lucy's for happy hour. You should come along and try to shake this off."

"Sounds like a plan." I was tempted to tell Bruce that I was waiting for a phone call because my drugged-out mother was afraid my cancer-ridden father had disappeared, and we had the cops out looking for him. It wasn't often that Bruce wasn't up my butt for something. But, he was a good mentor, and I was glad to finally be included in the after-work circle.

"You're going to be useless for the remainder of the afternoon. Wrap this up and I'll come back and get you. We'll go over together." He walked out. I looked up at the clock.

I called Jill and told her I was headed to Lucy's.

"What are you going to say in your response to the motion to dismiss?" she asked.

"The usual. You writing a piece on this? Don't quote me on any of it, Jill!"

"Don't worry, Abby, I already have what I need. Dad said that judge was a slippery one."

"Seriously? Why didn't you tell me? I never would have thought that about Judge Kehoe. How 'bout getting one of those sources of yours to find out what really happened? Throw me a bone here, Jill. Jeez."

"I bet you're not going to like what I find, but I'll see what I can do, Abs."

"How do you know…?"

"Listen, I've got to go. I'll see you soon." She hung up abruptly before I had time to ask her anything else.

CHAPTER 4

W e stood shoulder to shoulder up against the bar at Lucy's. "Come on, Abby, let's go outside!" Jill yelled and started moving through the crowd.

"You find out anything about the judge, Jill?" I took a big gulp of my fruity red drink. It was sweet, but strong.

"Gotta give me a little time. I'm good, but not that good," Jill said, and laughed.

Some of my coworkers had commandeered a tall sidewalk table and waved us over. The stars were gleaming over the streetlights. It was a particularly bright night. I introduced Jill to Bruce and some of the other DAs at my office, many of whom she already knew.

I felt my phone ring in my pocket. As I went to pick it up, Jill said, "Let it go, Abby."

"Can't, Jill. I've got some crazy shit happening at home." I recognized the number.

I stepped away to answer, "Jason, did you find him?"

All I could hear Jason say, was "Your dad…"

"What? What about Dad? You find him?" The music was too loud even outside the bar. "Let me call you right back. I can't hear you!" I screamed into my phone. I assumed they had probably found him out on Three Mile Harbor, fishing or something. I walked a little way down the street where it was darker, but I could still hear the lively hum of the night.

"Jesus, Abby, I've been trying to reach you for a half hour, and then you say you have to call back." Jason sounded frustrated, but there was softness in his voice, reminiscent of when we first met and were only friends. I wondered if we could erase all that happened and go back to when it was just like that.

"I'm out with the boss. I'm sorry. It's loud here. So, where was he? Three Mile Harbor? Montauk?"

"You need to come home. Get the first flight tomorrow morning. Tonight, if you can. Get yourself to the airport."

"What are you talking about? Where'd you find him?" I saw Jill headed up the street and waved her off.

"That's the thing, Abby. We found him in Sag Harbor. He jumped off the bridge and killed himself."

"I don't believe you. Please, tell me he's at the hospital…." I sat down on the curb in the dark.

"He drowned. I'm sorry, I don't know what else to say except you need to come home."

I let the words linger and felt my fun little buzz turn into nausea. "How could he do this to Mom?" was my first thought. Then I put the phone down, got on my knees, and threw up on the sidewalk.

"Abby, Abby, you still there?"

I pushed my hair back and picked up the phone, "Um, Jason, thanks. I'll call you back when I get my arrangements straight."

Jill ran over. "You okay Abby? Jeez, I didn't think you drank that much?" I motioned for her to sit down. I sat on the curb, wiped my mouth, and tried to compose myself.

"My, my, father just died," I stuttered, "I, I, I've got to call my mom. I have to go home…."

"Jesus, Abby, I'm sorry. I'll drive you to the airport, whatever you need."

"Help me figure out how to get home."

"Okay…" Jill put her arm around my shoulders. "I can loan you the money if you need, Abby. It's no big deal."

"Thanks, Jill. That's not it. I just can't believe it. I don't even know what to say." I put my head in my hands, but I couldn't cry; I felt so shell-shocked.

"We need to get you on a plane tonight, or tomorrow at the latest." Jill hugged me close.

We sat outside for a little while longer. The music from inside felt like it was vibrating the sidewalk. New Orleans and all its wildness made it easy to forget. A few minutes later, I went back over to the table.

I pulled Bruce aside and said, "I have a family emergency." He looked at me strangely, and I continued, "My father has died, and I need to go back up to New York. I'll call you from there on Monday and send you the details so that you can file the response to the motion to dismiss for me, if that's OK?" The words felt surreal, like a script coming out of my mouth. "What? What did you say?" Bruce looked at me quizzically and finished the rest of his beer. The music was loud, and we'd all had a few drinks already. I repeated what I'd told him, and he looked at me like *his* father had died. "Call me on Monday, and we'll figure out what to do with your caseload while you're away." And then he hugged me, holding me for a few extra seconds.

Jill grabbed my hand and pulled me toward the car, saying, "Come on Abby, we need to get going." I needed to get organized and let Jason know when he could pick me up.

* * *

I hadn't told Jason that I was moving away and going to law school until the day I broke up with him. We dated in high school, during college, and for the year I'd moved home after graduating.

Jason was going to stay in town and be a cop. He'd gone to Suffolk Community College, to the police academy, and then he'd scored a job in our hometown. He loved being a local cop and our plan was that I was going to move back home after college. Jason had saved enough money and bought a house and a dog. That summer after graduation I had my suspicions that he was cheating on me, so I started cheating on him with Johnny. I applied to law school with the thought that if I got in somewhere, I would break up with him, which was a stupid plan, but I didn't know how else to do it. He had told me I'd be nothing without him, and I was starting to believe him. Things with Johnny were heating up, but I was still with Jason and becoming paranoid that he would find out.

Johnny and I took a trip to New Orleans for Mardi Gras that year. I'd lied to Jason and told him I was going away with Val, which was exhilarating. For the first time in my life I was doing something bad. "Couldn't you see living here? Don't you love it?" We were sitting at a little table in the Café du Monde drinking *café au lait* and eating *beignets* and staring across the road at Jackson Square. Johnny agreed and continued to feed my fantasy that we'd go down together and start a life for ourselves while I was going to law school. When I mentioned my love of New Orleans to Jason, he'd said, "That shithole? Bunch of people on the take down there."

Then the drunk driving accident happened. Johnny went to jail when it should have been me. I could hardly live with myself, let alone Jason. I had to leave for law school in New Orleans and tried to forget about them both. There was nothing I could do for Johnny except hope that he'd be okay in there.

* * *

I went home, and Jill and I called every airline we could think of to arrange a flight back to New York in the morning. Bereavement fares were bullshit. I charged my credit card without flinching and picked the flight that left early but didn't get me back to Long Island until the late afternoon after two stopovers. I threw a few things in an overnight bag.

"Jill, you mind waking up early and driving me to the airport?"

"I could stay you know—I could sleep over," she said.

"That sounds good, Jill. That way at least one of us will wake up on time." I didn't want to be alone.

I changed into a T-shirt and shorts, grabbed a few Abita beers, went over to the couch, and sat down next to Jill, who was watching *Law & Order* reruns. We both stared at the TV and sipped our beers. During a commercial, she looked over at me and clicked off the sound.

"If you look at me like that, I'm going to cry." She grabbed me and held me while I cried until I was heaving, and then I stopped, exhausted. I got up to splash water on my face.

"You're strong, Abby, don't forget that." She handed me my beer as I sat back down on the couch.

"I've got to get a little sleep, or I'm going to be toast tomorrow." I gulped down the rest of my beer and I felt like I couldn't keep my eyes open.

"Let's get some rest," Jill said as she grabbed my hand and pulled me to my feet.

After I brushed my teeth, I grabbed two aspirin and a big glass of water. Then we climbed in, each claiming a side of my full-sized bed. I had the air-conditioning on so it was comfortable enough to sleep under my fluffy comforter with the French country duvet that my mother had sent me. The fresh smell of the detergent reminded me of my grandmother. I couldn't believe this was happening. If I had been with Val right now, I wouldn't have found out about this for weeks. We'd probably be diving off the coast of Thailand now. It happened to my friend Kara when her brother was killed in a car accident; she didn't find out until a week later. I was grateful that I could manage to come home without much of a problem.

I woke up abruptly. Jill moved but didn't wake up. I'd dreamt that all my teeth were falling out one by one, and I couldn't stop it. The clock said 2:57 a.m. and I had a few more hours to go. Licking my gums to make sure all my teeth were in place, I realized that I probably needed another aspirin.

When Jill dropped me off at the airport, she said, "It'll be okay, Abby. Call me if you need anything." She was still wearing her pajamas. "All of this will be waiting for you when you get back." She gestured to my old Honda like one of the girls on *The Price is Right*.

"I'll call you. Don't get too comfy in my bed. When your AC starts working again I'm sending you back uptown," I said as I hugged her. I started thinking about how Bruce would handle Darcy and the case, and decided I'd call him when things settled a bit. It wasn't like I was going to be gone forever.

"We'd like to invite all of our passengers in Zone 3 to board at this time," a woman said over the loudspeaker as everyone shuffled themselves and their bags to the gate. I was in-between a mother with a babbling five-year-old, his grandmother, and a man in his fifties talking rapidly on his cellphone, trying to get in a morning meeting. I wanted to yell, "Dad committed suicide!" just to make it feel real.

As I walked down the corridor to board, I stared at a picture that I thought might be Thailand and thought of Val. I pushed my sunglasses back up over the bridge of my nose and shifted the black pea coat over my carry-on. My mother had given me the coat for Christmas last year instead of the coffee maker that I'd suggested. She said it would never go out of style. Later, when I reached into the pocket, I found thirty bucks with a Christmas tag tied to it.

"Wouldn't it be nice to go there instead of a holiday in New

York?" The grandmother in front of me was rambling, stepping back beside me as her daughter and the child went ahead.

"I'm not going on a vacation," my voice cracked, and I took a deep breath.

"I used to travel a lot before my grandkids. It's such a wonderful experience. I encouraged my daughter to do that before she got married just as I'd suggest you might do too," she smiled as she talked. She almost looked too young to be a grandma, with her jeans topped by a shirt with a blazer and her silver locks pulled back in a ponytail. The only thing that gave her away were her hands, which were swollen with arthritis at the joints of her fingers. Her grandson ran back to her and grabbed her hand, and she walked forward with him before I had a chance to ask her anything else. I sipped the last bit of my iced coffee and moved forward so I was right behind them again.

The woman turned back again to me as the mother crouched down explaining something about the Empire State Building to the boy. "This is my first trip with my grandson. If we can do New York then we can do anywhere, don't you think?"

I shook my head.

"I don't mean to be nosy, but are you okay Miss?"

"You ever do something unforgivable?" The words spilled out of my mouth and my eyes filled with tears.

She looked stunned and said, "We all have things we regret but nothing that can't be fixed. It'll be okay, sweetie." She touched my elbow and turned away. I'd never spoken to anyone about the DWI accident with Johnny and how it was my fault.

The line lurched forward and the chipper attendants waved the mother and the rest of us to our seats. I sat down, closed my eyes, and tried to fall asleep, but I couldn't. My mind kept flashing to my father and what I wished I had told him before he died.

CHAPTER 5

I t was hard to miss Jason's Mets cap and sturdy build through the crowd. When I finally reached him, he took my bag and said, "Man, this sucks. I'm so sorry. Flight okay?"

"Well, a snooze and a nice little cry while watching a ridiculously stupid movie that I can't even remember the name of made the flight pretty uneventful. Thanks for doing this."

"Your dad was the best, and no matter what's happened between us, this just sucks. And Christ, your mom can't pick you up. And your sister, forget it! Not a big deal to help you get home for this." He gave me one of his hugs that made me want to curl up and be with him forever, and then I shuddered, trying hard to suck back my tears.

I breathed deeply, gently pushing him away and said, "I just have the carry-on. Did you get a good parking spot?"

"I always get a good spot." He gave me a wink and handed me a fleece jacket he'd brought along.

"I have my coat Mom sent me." He shrugged and handed me a bottle of water. I took a swig.

"Switched to the late shift so I could get you and have a little time to hang for a bit."

"I probably have a little time before Corrine gets there, but I'm worried about Mom." I knew my sister would be arriving from the city with the kids and the nanny and lots of luggage. She'd married both the nicest and richest guy in the world but had managed to become a complete snob. I started calling her Commandina instead of Corrine. I told her I liked her better when she was awkward and funny. Now she had turned into one of those summer people we used to joke about.

"Johnny is out of jail, so I'd expect we're both going to see him," he blurted.

"Anyone see him yet? Have you spoken with him?" I felt uneasy talking to Jason about him. I didn't want him to get angry especially when he was being so nice to me.

"Listen, just don't say anything to him. Better if you just stay away."

"It's not like we kept in touch." Jason and I certainly wouldn't be his first call on the outside.

"What's done is done, so don't go all righteous on me and let him know that we set him up."

"I never should have let you talk me into that. It's not right, it wasn't right." I turned away from him and crossed my arms, thinking back to that night…

* * *

The night of the accident was confusing and felt like a nightmare. I must have blacked out because when I came to when I was on a stretcher, getting loaded into the ambulance. My head felt wet, but when I tried to reach my hand up I realized I was completely strapped in.

"Where's Johnny?" I slurred. The lights in the back of the ambulance made me wince, and I knew something bad had happened. Jason was sitting next to me.

"Just keep quiet, Abby," he whispered. "I hate you right now and think you're an asshole, but I'm not going to let you go down for this."

"What are you talking about?" The last thing I remembered was having drinks at the bar and dancing. Then I was blank.

"Trust me, I'm keeping them away from you, so just keep quiet and follow my lead. Johnny was driving the car when you crashed, and you both killed someone."

"Oh my God," I gasped when I said this. I wanted to take it back. "But it was my car, I was…" I remembered the lights, trying to focus on the road and shuddered at the impact.

"You weren't driving. I was following you guys and moved Johnny behind the wheel."

"Why did you…?"

"It's too late now. They're arresting him at the hospital. You asked me to do it, Abby. What the hell was I supposed to do?"

* * *

I snapped back to present when Jason poked my arm and said, "You still owe me one." I didn't want to talk about it because it wouldn't do either of us any good—nothing would change. I didn't like feeling beholden to Jason and it made me feel guiltier for what had happened.

I called home to let them know I'd arrived. My sister's husband, James, answered and told me, "We'll be fine until you get here. No rush." I could hear the commotion in the background.

"You mind stopping for a quick bite? I'm starving," I said to Jason.

"I know a little diner we can hit. You look like you could use something to eat." We pulled over at a brightly lit joint not far from JFK. I ordered a bottle of wine and hadn't realized he wasn't drinking until I was halfway done with it.

"Can I come over and see Jack for a bit?" Jack was the chocolate lab that I'd bought Jason our last Christmas together. Jason said he was *our baby*, or at least good practice until we had our own. I loved Jack but the only thing that dog was practice for was getting another dog.

"I don't know if that's such a good idea, Abby."

"I promise I won't stay long."

"It's not a good idea, Abby."

* * *

The first time Jason and I got together was the night of our senior prom. Val, Jason, and I decided to go as a trio. We got Jason's cousin, Zach, to drive us around in Jason's dad's classic car so we could look cool. Val and I had tropical wine coolers and screwdrivers. Jason made the screwdrivers into a drink he called a "Saturn." He used coffee filters so when he poured the vodka it floated on top and was a shot with a chaser.

It wasn't much different than the Saturday nights hanging out in Jason's mom's Country Squire wagon. Zach had a beard so we made him go into the deli and get baby food and wine coolers or beer, while complaining about his drive in from the city.

Then, after the prom, we cruised to the beach with the rest of our class. Zach and Val went down on the beach to the bonfire. We stayed up at the car and made more Saturns so we could finish the last song on our favorite Rolling Stones tape, and we started making out. We'd kissed before, but this was different. We became boyfriend and girlfriend after that night, and Val was a little pissed at us.

* * *

Jason pulled the car into a wooded area and turned off the ignition. "Do you want to talk for a minute before I drop you off?"

"I don't think we have anything else to talk about, do you?" My heart was palpitating the same way it was before the trial—my head felt like it was going to burst, and I started heaving.

"I just, this just all feels so unreal to me...." Jason turned toward me and I buried my head into the nook between his head and shoulder. He whispered that it was going to be okay. I wasn't sure if I could handle the next few days. I lifted my head up and kissed him—our sex had always been better when I was angry or upset. Through my tears, I lifted my head and leaned into him. He kissed me hard.

"We shouldn't," I whispered, but that just made him moan.

"Shhhh...." He pushed his hands down my pants.

I undid my seatbelt. "Take this off," he said and pulled off my shirt. He smelled like fresh-cut grass.

I opened my mouth to say something and he put his finger on my lips, then lifted me up on top of him.

As soon as we were finished he said, "Shit, I need to get out of here and get you home."

"What time does your shift start?"

"I've got some stuff to do beforehand," he said, fixing his shirt and zipping up his jeans.

"Can I borrow your old car while I'm here?" I asked.

"Don't have that beater anymore but I'll see if I can't get you a loner from someone. I'll call you if I do."

He pulled up in front of my house. I grabbed my bag and said, "I'll see you, okay?"

"Just don't say anything stupid if you see him. I know you and what you're thinking."

"I doubt I'll even run into him, so just shut up about it," I said. And with that Jason sped off. I felt like I had to run upstairs and get in the shower.

When I came through the door, I was surprised that my mom was cooking like it was Thanksgiving, buzzing around the kitchen.

"Hey, what's going on around here? Can I help?" Mom stopped mid-stride and came over and gave me a hug. Her face looked drawn, her eyes were glassy.

"I'm just glad that you're home," she said and went back to cooking without another word. I went over to the sink and started cleaning up all the dirty pots and pans. The only noise for the next hour was of pans clanking and the water running. I stood at the sink while Mom moved all over the kitchen. The sauce she was making smelled delicious, as did the roast. I moved behind her to see what she was doing and put my hand on her back. She lifted the spoon and put it to my mouth after blowing on it.

"This is wonderful. Dad would have approved," I said. She turned her face and went back to stirring the pot. Tears streamed down her cheeks. "I'm sorry, I didn't mean to make you cry."

"Cooking makes me feel better," was all she could say. I stepped back to the sink and continued cleaning things up.

She sat down at the kitchen table, and I sat down next to her. She put her hand on mine; I could feel her trembling.

"Where are Corrine and the kids?"

"They went to pick up more food. I told the nanny to get them out of here for a bit and leave me alone for a while. Oh, Abby, I don't know if I can do this." She grabbed the bottle of pills in the middle of the table, opened it, and popped two in her mouth.

"You know, if he'd just told me how much pain he was in I could have helped him. We talked about assisted suicide, but I said I didn't think I could go through with it. Now look what he's done!" She slumped in the chair and pushed her hair back from her eyes. She'd gotten a lot grayer since I'd seen her last. She refused to dye her hair and it was growing in a lovely salt and pepper.

"Maybe that's why he did it himself…so you wouldn't have to go through with it?"

"It's a sin," she whispered. I could tell by the slur of her words that the pills were taking effect quickly. "He was always protecting me." She took a tissue out of her pocket along with two little red pills, popped them in her mouth, then blew her nose. "This is not how things were supposed to turn out for us."

"It's going to be okay, Mom. I promise." I grabbed her hand and gave it a squeeze. She wiped her eyes and looked at me as if she could see right through my heart.

* * *

Pulling out my mother's photographs of her exotic trips with her friends was one of my favorite memories. "Let's go to Rome today," she'd say. My sister would get out the *Encyclopedia Britannica*, and I would go to the bookshelf in Dad's office and get the old travel books and the photos. Mom would go to her drawers to find her Roman souvenirs and bring us silk scarves to wear around our heads in case it was windy on our trip to Rome.

"You know, girls, it was impossible to cross the street in Rome unless you were pretty. The cars would honk and keep going—they might even bump a lady."

"Did they stop for you, Mommy?" we asked.

"Oh, I wish I had a picture of it!" She laughed, and we watched her eyes dance with the memory. "You girls have to promise me you'll go there when you're older and tell me if it's the same. They would definitely stop for both of you!" We promised. We'd spend an hour looking up pictures and quizzing Mommy from what we could find in the encyclopedia and the travel books. She'd tell us the one true way to figure out who you are is to see the world and learn about how others live. "Take what you like from your travels and bring it into your own life," she'd said. After a while, she'd leave us alone to go into the kitchen and make spaghetti marinara so we could have the full Italian experience. She laughed when we'd say, "*Bravissimo*" about the spaghetti or "*Ciao Mama*" when we went to bed. She and Dad never had the kind of money to go on the type of trips she used to go on. Instead of answering us when we asked about that, she'd say, "Plenty of time to get married, so make sure you travel the world before you do."

* * *

We heard the yelling and commotion before my sister and her posse even came into the house. Mom was staring at the stove, attempting to finish cooking, and I was drying the dishes and putting them away.

"Aunt Abby, Aunt Abby!" My nephews, Brooke and Casey, ran over and wrapped their arms around my legs. "Grandpa died."

"I know, guys, I know."

"Grandma said he's up in heaven, and we can still talk to him but not on the phone." Mom smiled when they said this. My sister's kids tended to drive me nuts. Corrine and James practiced what they called a "continuation" of their kids' Montessori school. They felt that meant letting the kids do whatever they wanted and that they would learn their own boundaries. I didn't think that was how a Montessori school was supposed to work, but if I tried to say something, Corrine would rip my head off.

"What did you bring us?" Brooke whined. "Yeah, what did you bring us?" said Casey, who started running around in circles, then fell in the middle of the floor.

"Nothing this time, guys, except tickles!" I pretended I was a monster and dashed after them as they squealed and ran away.

"Boys, time to come with me," said Heike, Corrine's German live-in nanny, and the boys stopped in their tracks.

"It's okay, Heike, they can stay for a bit," I said.

"It's better if they go with her," Corrine said and pointed to Heike to take them outside.

"Are you sure, Corrine? I never get to see them..."

Corrine looked at me and said, "You look terrible and your face is all splotchy. Let them go."

"You look like you've gained about ten pounds," I said and walked back into the kitchen. I could feel Corrine seething, but I didn't care. She'd started it.

"We need to go to the funeral parlor to make arrangements. I was waiting for you," she huffed as she tried to bring down her tone of voice.

"Mom, do you want to come with us?" I asked.

"Sounds like you girls need some time together without me," she said and shook her head as she continued chopping vegetables.

Corrine barked, "Mom, leave it. Heike can take care of the rest of the cooking if you'll just please go pop a DVD in for the kids." Mom nodded and walked away. "Jamie dear, please go to the store again if we are missing anything around here. It's like she hasn't been shopping in days." Corrine tugged my shirt and pointed toward the door.

I didn't want to argue anymore. I knew how she could be and she'd gotten worse since she'd gotten her big fat managing director job at some big bank. Initially, when she'd gotten together with James, she'd said she'd never need to work again. She stopped for a few months after they had Casey, but then she said she was just too bored to only be a mom.

When we got in the car, Corrine said, "Let's get a drink before we go over."

"We can stop by McSorley's. It's on the way," I said.

We sat at the stools in the dark bar. "Two doubles of Jameson," she told the bartender. He brought us two short glasses and poured amber-looking liquid from a square bottle that was not Jameson. I watched her look at the bottle and then dig into her purse for a twenty, slapping it up on the bar. After he poured, we clinked our glasses together and drank down our shots in one big gulp.

"Another," she said. He poured again. In the meantime, she told me about their new 'penthouse with a view' that they were renovating and the crazy decorator, John Sebastian. He'd convinced her that all a home needed to be unique was imported white marble, fresh flowers as well as objects he'd amassed from antique stores that looked like they could have come from an estate sale, which was a fancier way of saying garage sale in my book.

"If it's expensive then it must be stylish, right?" I joked. She punched me in the arm and we both laughed.

"What about you? Any big cases to talk about? You a big hotshot yet?" She said as she gulped the remainder of the last shot.

"I did just finish with this case I had thought was going to be the big one, but then it really got messed up. There was this girl who got raped and the guy, well, the guy was a real scumbag, but with an influential family. All I can say is that I don't even know what happened. The judge got arrested, and as soon as I get back I have to try to put things back together again, but I don't even know if I can."

"The judge got arrested? How is that even possible?"

"I honestly don't know and I can't do anything from here anyway. It's a real mess," I said.

"Something will work out for you, Abby. It always does, you know."

"Thanks, Corrine, I hope so. We'd better get going, huh?"

By the time we got to the funeral home, I was feeling a little woozy from the shots. We walked into what felt like someone's grandma's living room. The funeral director was a sixty-something guy in a black pinstriped suit, with his hair slicked back like one of the bandmembers of the Stray Cats.

"*So* sorry to hear about your loss. Do you know what you are looking for? How many days do you want to have services? We have a lot of nice products to make your dad feel real comfortable," he rambled, but all I could focus on was the overpowering smell of onions coming from him.

"Why don't you just show us the coffins, and we can work from there," Corrine said and punched me in the thigh, which made me hop out of my seat.

He led us up to the second floor of the house, which had many bedroom doors. He went up to the middle door and opened it. It looked like all the bedroom walls had been taken down to form one very expansive room—of coffins. He flicked on the lights, which made the room as bright as an auto showroom.

"Let's start over here," he said and showed us a fancy one, blue with chrome on it and lots of padding that looked like a comfortable couch. "Stays intact and doesn't erode." He knocked on the side of the coffin and it echoed.

"I don't think so," I said and looked at Corrine, who was digging into her purse.

Then he brought us over to a dark maroon one. "This one is like a Maserati. Your dad liked cars, didn't he?"

"What about the pine plank ones, have any of those?" Corrine started laughing hysterically, gasping for air. But then, she started to cry. Her face turned red, and she started to shake.

"Um, well, those are just for people who…"

"Why don't you give us some time to look things over?" I put my arm around Corrine and she gently brushed me away and walked to the back of the room by the windows.

"Take your time," he said and walked quickly to the door.

I went over to Corrine, who was starting to calm down. "You okay?"

She looked up at me and couldn't get any words out. With her gasping, I couldn't tell if she was laughing or crying. Then she said, "Maybe he'd like one in the shape of a fishing boat?" Corrine started to choke on her tears and sat down on the floor. I sat down next to her and put my arm around her. Instead of pushing me away, she put her head on my shoulder.

"It's too weird, isn't it? We shouldn't be here," I said, as tears streamed down my cheeks.

"It's better this way. Anything ever happens to me, I'm giving you permission to pull the plug. Promise me, okay?" She blew her nose and perked up again.

"So long as you promise me too." Then, like we had done when we were kids sharing a room, we locked our pinkies together and flapped our hands like a butterfly, like we had done about a million times before. We sat there in silence for a few minutes in the middle of the room, where the light shined on a lacquered black coffin with fancy silver handles, the Rolls, I'm sure. The guy came back into the room, looked at us, and then walked back out.

"It's all right," Corrine yelled after him, "We're ready now." He came back in.

"What about that one back there?" I stood up and pointed to the simple maple wood box tucked away in the far corner of the room, past the blue Lexus, the Maserati, and the cheesy white Camry.

"That looks perfect, just what Dad would have wanted," Corrine agreed. The director walked over to the blue coffin and took some paperwork out from inside the box.

"We don't want the Lexus. That's the one we want." I pointed to the simple maple box that was still very much an upgrade from pine planks. If there was a statement to be made, this was the one we wanted to make, dollar value aside.

"Let's head back downstairs and get started with the rest of the details," he said. His voice was almost melancholy.

Back in Mr. Onion Breath's cramped office, we decided on days, times, and all the accoutrements that go with giving a full-on wake: the mass cards, a sign-in book, and a few other things he insisted we needed since we were too exhausted to argue. We declined a few things and he scrunched his nose at us. "Have a check ready for the full amount when I see you next," he said as we stood up to leave. Corrine grabbed my elbow and led me out before I could say anything else.

"Come on, Abby, let's go!" I could hear the boisterous yell of my dad even when I was out in midfield in the middle of a soccer game. "Fight for it! Fight for it!" I was ten, one of the smallest players, and one of two girls on the team; he wanted me to be tough.

"You're just as good as those guys, Abby. Sometimes you must play smarter," he'd said one day when I had gotten nailed by one of the fullbacks on the other team and missed an opportunity for a goal. A foul was called, but then I choked and it went out of bounds. At least I didn't cry.

"Don't let them intimidate you. Don't ever let anyone do that to you." The next time I brought the ball down the field, I made sure I had my elbows out, and then, before the fullback came at me, I faked right. Then I passed to Jimmy, the center forward, and he scored! After that, whenever I got scared of anything, I thought of my dad that day and let his words run through my head.

After dropping Corrine off at the house, I headed to Finnegan's Pub and ordered a shot of Jameson and a half pint of Harp. I didn't recognize the barman or anyone else at the bar. The shot stung before it felt warm on the back of my throat.

The barman poured me another and said, "Sure sorry to hear about your dad."

I looked up and muttered, "Thanks."

"You look like him. He used to come in here after fishing and talk about you and your sister. Real nice man."

He walked over to the other side of the bar and started talking to a guy about the basketball game on TV. The second shot gave me that mild spinning feeling that made me feel like I was at Café Mogador listening to someone try to channel the likes of one of the old swampy-blues singers down in The Marigny. I wished my dad could have come down to New Orleans and seen my new life. Maybe he would have had some good ideas about the case and the judge or maybe even what to do about Darcy.

"Hey, you okay?" I hadn't noticed, but the old guy that had been watching ESPN had sidled up to me.

"I'm fine, thanks," I said and stared straight back down into my drink. His wrinkled face and silvery blue eyes reminded me of Charlie, my dad's best friend. Charlie was a quiet man, except for when he was with my dad. I suppose it was because he spent so much time on the water by himself. My dad always said, "That Charlie, now there's a true salt. Not too many pinhookers left in this part of the world." Charlie always said that only by using a rod and reel could you truly call yourself a fisherman. I pictured my dad fishing, tossing out the line with Charlie today.

A few times a year, Charlie would let my dad go to work with him. My dad came back so happy, my mom used to tease him that maybe he should switch professions. He'd laugh and toss her the dinner that he usually got as payment if they caught enough that day. If it was a bad day, then the whole catch belonged to the boat. But the days when Charlie and Dad would catch double- or triple-headers on the line, well, those were the days that we got dinner for at least one, maybe two nights. "Tastes better when you catch it yourself," he'd say, or, "God was electrocuting the water, those fish were jumping so high today."

"Don't beat yourself up too much," the man said, jolting me back from my memory.

"I had no idea he was going to kill himself," I said. I motioned to the barman to give us both another shot.

"He was probably sicker than he let on to anyone."

"How would you know?"

"He'd come in here occasionally with that friend of his, that young cop, Jason. You know, the one that always wears the Mets hat. He seemed like a kind man. I'm sure…"

"Thanks, that means a lot, but I don't want to talk about this anymore." I poured the shot down my throat and shook my head, swaying on the chair.

"You alright? Need a ride home?" the man asked.

I shook my head again and said, "I'm fine." I threw my money up on the bar. The bartender pushed twenty back at me. I stumbled to the bathroom and sat down and cried for a minute. I splashed some water on my face and then left out the back door.

The parking lot was sparsely lit. I tripped on the sidewalk and fell to the ground, scraping my knee. I screamed up at the sky, "Why? Why?" My stomach lurched, and I rolled over on my side and puked. I sat there for another minute heaving. I was angry, angry at my dad for not giving us a chance to help him, and I was irritated he'd been palling around with Jason.

"Goddamn it!" I mumbled, sitting up. I stumbled over to my car. I sat down in the driver's seat for a minute and tried to breathe. I pulled out of the parking lot and onto Main Street and turned the radio up. It was one of those popular songs that stuck in your head but still had a good beat. I saw flashing red lights behind me. I pulled to the side of the road and fumbled in my purse, trying to find my wallet to get my license.

When the cop shined the light in my face, I was sure I was completely screwed.

"What the hell are you doing?"

"Uh, Jason, how did you know it was me?" I was even more nervous than if it had just been any old cop.

"Your family is worried about you and sent me looking for you. You're getting wasted? What do you think? Killing yourself or somebody else is the answer? Didn't you learn from what happened to Johnny? Are you some kind of idiot?" He opened the door of the car and I winced again. "Get out of the car and get in the back."

"You're arresting me?" I choked, coughing until I puked again on the side of the road.

"Jesus, Abby, hurry up or you're going to get us both in trouble. I should arrest you, but just get in the damn car."

"I don't want to."

"You don't have a goddamned choice!" He grabbed onto my arm and shoved me into the back seat.

Jason mumbled something to his dispatcher, and I sunk back into the cool leather seats that had a whiff of smoke on them. I lay down and rolled myself into a ball. Finnegan's was a dumb choice if I didn't want to be found. It was where the three of us used to hang out when Val wasn't off exploring the world.

I decided that after Darcy's case was exhausted, hopefully in our favor, I was going to head to Thailand to catch up with Val for a few weeks to figure out who I was and what I wanted to do with my life. I tried to think of why my dad would have gone to such an extreme. It was driving me crazy. Dad had to have shared something with Charlie.

CHAPTER 6

I woke up with a screaming headache, but with the realization that my father was dead and wasn't coming back again. I couldn't help myself. I sobbed for a few minutes, then went to the bathroom to splash my face. I hoped I could hold it together. I tried not to think about Darcy and what was going on but I couldn't help it and it was ripping me up.

Wakes are weird, sort of like going to a wax museum and finding someone you know. Nobody looked like themselves when filled with formaldehyde, dressed in their Sunday best, and otherwise unnaturally coiffed by the funeral parlor. When I was six, a similar scene had been so confusing to me that my grandmother told me to touch the body when nobody was looking. It's something I'd done ever since.

"She feels like a Barbie doll, but an old one," I'd said at my Aunt Colleen's funeral. Everyone in earshot broke out in laughter. Touching the body that felt "like an old Barbie" had become a family joke, especially during the holidays. But I had never stopped doing it. I'd even touch strangers given the chance.

I knew no one would mind if I touched my father. In fact, maybe they would expect it, and it would make them smile. Mom, Corrine, and I disagreed about the open casket.

Corrine huffed, pouring herself a glass of wine and said, "Fine, you want everyone to see him like that and gawk, go ahead. I'm going upstairs to take a bath."

"You do that and we'll take care of everything. You just relax up there." I didn't want to fight, but found myself welling up with tears. Corrine treated everyone like we were her hired help or underlings. It drove me crazy. But, we weren't teenagers anymore, and I didn't have to follow her rules.

* * *

I couldn't live her lifestyle even if I wanted to. The one time I tried in New Orleans, I got duped. One year, a friend's father, a member of the Krewe of Bacchus, gave us tickets to the Mardi Gras Bacchus ball at the Performing Arts Center. My friend got sick but told me I should go anyhow with someone else. Jill and I spent a few hours doing our hair and makeup, and getting all dressed up. I wore the only floor-length gown I owned. We arrived at the party, tickets in hand. We had a few cocktails, but there was no food. When they served the King Cake we each took a large piece and brought it back to an empty table and noticed that everyone was sitting down, looking out at the stage.

"You are going to love this…" Jill whispered. I shrugged, thinking there'd be some sort of parade or Mardi Gras display. Eight teenaged girls came out onstage in big white poufy dresses. If I hadn't known any better, I would have thought it was a multiple wedding for the Moonies.

"This is a debutante ball?" I whispered back to Jill incredulously.

"Think anyone will notice if we sneak out?" Jill nudged me and pointed to the entranceway. The girls who had been taking tickets at the doorway were now closer to the dance floor, gawking at the debutantes.

"Did you know it was going to be a debutante ball? Were you ever a debutante?"

Jill scoffed. "Trust me. I tried not to go to these things. You really wanted to go to this party so who was I to ruin your big night out so you could see what you've been missing all your life?"

"Let's hit the Columns. Shame to waste all our effort in getting all gussied up," I said.

"Sounds good to me, so long as we make a quick pit stop on the way over. I can't survive these drinks on King Cake." Jill laughed. We ran to the car and pulled out our up-dos while stopped at the Rally's drive-through. We scarfed down a burger and fries and tried not to drip any grease on our dresses.

As we walked up the stairs to the Columns Bar, we could see the warm candlelight illuminating a girl in a long pink dress playing the cello in a jazz trio that was playing in the corner of the bar. We sat at a table near a couple of fraternity-looking guys and ordered our first round of vodka tonics.

One of them ventured over after our first round. "What are you ladies drinking?" "Whatever you guys are buying," Jill joked.

I'm not too sure what happened over the next few hours, but we both went back to their place. We ended up doing the tramp trot the next morning with our long dresses and bare feet, shoes in hand.

"Very classy," I said to Jill, feeling very undebutante-like with my hair in disarray.

"You are pretty much indoctrinated now. This is how the upper crust does it," she said and laughed. Luckily, the boys didn't live far from the bar, and we had snuck out before they woke up....

* * *

I headed upstairs to get changed for the wake. "Corrine," I called from the door of the bathroom, "can I borrow a sweater or something?" I cracked open the door. She had her eyes closed and was lying back in the tub with her big glass of red wine nearly empty on the tile floor.

"I brought a few extra sweaters. Figured you might need something coming up from the Deep South and all." She said this with an exaggerated Southern drawl, which made us both start to laugh.

"Cool, thanks." I was grateful.

"You know, it's like near impossible for someone to kill themselves jumping off that bridge. Heck, I did it in high school. And if I did it, then it's no big deal."

"Corrine, there's no evidence of foul play here, and Dad wrote a note, which is crazy, but I guess he was just really depressed." I felt guilty when I said this, like I should have seen it coming. Maybe I should have been home, and I could have prevented it.

"Don't look that way, Abby. There's nothing you could have done."

"I should have talked to him more. The last time I spoke with him, I told him I'd call him back, and then it got too late, so I didn't."

"Listen, if anyone should have seen it coming, it was me. I mean, I'm right here; I'm out all the time with the kids. We can't feel guilty about this, it's just one of those screwed-up things that's no one's fault."

"I know you're right, but I just can't stop thinking about it." I kept ruminating over the chicken-scratch note he left.

"Not too long ago, he asked me about when I jumped off the bridge. Then, he started to laugh, saying he and Charlie had joked about smoking pot for the cancer and then jumping off the bridge. I couldn't stop laughing at the thought of them passing a joint." Corrine hung over the tub and took the last swig of her wine, put it back down and dunked her head under the water.

"You know, it's weird that Charlie hasn't been around. But I'd just figured he was working on the boat and couldn't make it sooner," I said.

"Let's ask him tonight. I don't want to worry about this more than we should. You'd better get dressed. We don't have a lot of time!"

I went to Corrine's room and started looking through her things to see what would go with the black pants I'd brought along. I found a pretty blouse and a baby blue cashmere sweater. She came into the room with a big white towel wrapped around her.

"Okay if I use this?" I held them up for her to see. She nodded and shooed me out of the room.

As I got dressed in my old room, I looked around at some of my things still hung up from high school. There was a map of the world and some old photos of Val, Jason, and me next to a stack of CDs that I hadn't listened to in years. I thought of my new life in New Orleans and how happy I was to have made it out of here. Even if I wasn't on the trip with Val right now, I'm sure there'd be a postcard or two waiting for me when I got back to New Orleans. She had to have made it to India by now. Our plan had been to land in Delhi, head up to Agra to see the Taj Mahal, and then travel though Jaipur and then maybe try to get to Varanasi. Instead, I was going to a funeral. I had so many unanswered questions I hardly knew where to start.

When we got to the funeral home, there were swarms of people. I smiled at the sight of them. As I stepped inside, there was a hum of conversation. I talked to what seemed like every person who walked in the door and for a moment forgot about everything else except my family. Corrine stayed close to Mom, who was doing a decent job of holding things together. I was doing fine, too, until I saw Johnny standing in the back of the room. My stomach sank. He caught my eye and gave me a small grin. I nodded my head to the right, toward the side door. I felt a little sweaty and had no idea about what to say. I was touched that he'd shown up. I pushed my hair behind my right ear and grabbed a tissue to wipe the shine away from my brow. He was wearing a red T-shirt that was a little tight and accentuated his chest, which was more muscular than I remembered.

When he got closer, I reached out to touch his arm and squeezed it. "Hey, thanks for coming," I said.

"I wanted to tell you how sorry I was to hear about your dad and that I'm not mad at you anymore," he said quickly, as if he'd been practicing. He put his arms around me and I felt my body pulse. I stepped back and took a deep breath.

"How long have you been back?" I said, and then felt stupid for saying so, since Jason had told me he was back. I glanced to the back of the room to make sure that Jason wasn't here to witness us reconnecting.

"I got paroled a few weeks ago. I'm surprised you didn't hear."

As he said this, I stared. His hair was sexy, a little shorter than his chin, like it'd grown out a bit. He was wearing dark jeans and flip-flops, just like he always did no matter how cold it was.

"Been working in New Orleans. I'm a lawyer now. Dad was the one who really kept me posted about what was going on in town," I rambled.

"You look good, Abby. I'm glad I got to see you," he said, and turned to walk away.

I grabbed his arm again and said, "Listen, Johnny, I'm sorry. I bailed on you, and I am such a shit for that. I can't even believe you came here. What I did was wrong...."

He looked at me for what felt like a minute and deadpanned, "Well, you know what happens in prison, I found the Lord, and I think that's what led me back to you."

"Uh, okay...."

"I'm kidding, you fool, but I gotcha for a second, didn't I?" He smiled and tried not to laugh. I punched him in the shoulder and tilted my head to the door. I wanted to go outside and talk privately without anyone looking at us.

"You got me good. And God knows I needed the laugh." I felt giddy; he made me nervous.

"Don't get me wrong, I'm no heathen, but I didn't turn into a Bible beater. Don't worry." He smiled in the way he did when I met him that had made my knees weak.

"Jason told me that you were out." I looked at the ground when I said this, knowing it made me look like an idiot. "He picked me up at the airport."

"You're never going to learn, are you? Not that it's any of my business, especially now, but you need to stay away from that guy." He pushed my hair back and then put his hand on my shoulder.

All I wanted to do was lean into him and have him put his arms around me and pretend nothing had changed between us, but I babbled, "I'm working at the DA's office. In fact, I had this big case that ended in a mistrial the same day this happened. And then I had to come here and…"

"Why'd you stop writing to me?" He didn't seem angry, but hurt.

"I felt too guilty that you went to jail and after a while I just didn't know what to say and then time went by and I felt like an asshole. I didn't know what to say and it didn't feel fair that I was getting on with my life." I wanted to tell him that I thought about him constantly but that I needed to forget what happened.

"Well, I was driving so you were just dumb enough to be my passenger. What I did was stupid and wrong."

"Listen, after you finish up here, I could pick you up and we could go have a drink, talk about this somewhere else?" I was afraid any minute my mother or Corrine was going to see me, and then they'd start in on me about the accident and how I shouldn't associate with Johnny after what happened.

"No big deal, but I don't drink anymore. You know, the 12 Steps and stuff, been two years but now that I'm out it's different, but I want to keep it up. Been going to meetings and it's been a good way to connect now that I'm out."

"That's cool," I said. I remembered him telling me about the wine they used to make in their cells from fermenting fruit that tasted terrible, but it gave you a wicked buzz.

"Listen, I'd love to meet at our spot just to talk. Do you think you'd have any time? I'm driving my dad's red Toyota, but I really shouldn't be, so we'll have to make it short. I know some folks have an eye on me." He looked right through me and squeezed my shoulder gently.

"I'll have about an hour after the wake before I'll need to get back for dinner, so let's meet fifteen minutes after I leave. Sound good?" I hadn't been back to our spot since we were together. It was a hidden cove down a dead-end street. We could park there and then walk over the dunes to the ocean. We'd made love there for the first time. He'd had a bunch of beach blankets in the back of his car and we'd dragged them out to look at the stars one night. I hadn't yet pulled the trigger to break up with Jason, but we should have been broken up, since all we did was fight and I thought he might be cheating on me. Johnny gave me that butterfly feeling in a way that I never had felt. I wanted him to kiss me again right there and thankfully he took his hand back or I might have.

"Why don't you have a boyfriend?" he asked me one night when we were spread out on a blanket down by the ocean. It was close to midnight. I'd met up with him after a catering party he'd worked and I'd lied to Jason that I was working late, too, even though they hadn't needed me that night. Val would vouch for me.

"Can't we talk about something else?" I didn't want to lie any more than I already had. I got up from the blanket and ran down to the water and got my feet wet. I ran back up to dry sand and starting stripping off my clothes. Nothing was more exhilarating than jumping in the ocean at night with only the moonlight and the stars. You could sense the pulse of the ocean, catching the waves that you could feel, but couldn't see coming.

"Are you crazy?" Johnny came running after me. He tried to grab me, but I was too quick. I ran with abandon into the ocean, diving on top of the first wave.

"Chicken!" I knew I was being a tease, and I'd escalated the game we were playing by being naked. Before tonight, we had basically done everything but full-blown sex. I'd held back because I hadn't broken up with Jason yet, and felt like sex would be the ultimate in line-crossing. The water felt a little bit tingly, but it was refreshing on a warm August night.

I dove under another wave, and then I felt his hands run over my body. "Don't think you can get away so easily—I have night vision." I pressed myself against him and we floated over some of the waves until a set came in that we had to dive under. I grabbed his hand, and he brought me back to our blanket. I didn't even think about the fact that I was dodging my own rule. I could no longer say I wasn't cheating on Jason; it was too late for that.

* * *

Tonight was different. After I'd left the funeral parlor and said goodbye to the final people straggling out, I found myself waiting for Johnny, nervous that he wouldn't show up. I wondered if he'd gotten in trouble for driving and couldn't meet. I deserved to be stood up, I told myself, and started the car. I didn't need to desert my family on a day like today even if Johnny did deserve a big apology. And then he pulled up in his dad's little red pickup truck, just like he said. I smiled. But Johnny didn't look happy; he didn't look happy at all.

CHAPTER 7

J ohnny drove up and parked close to me, almost touching the reeds that hid the little pond that we had found so many years ago. The little sandy road had been grown over a bit by reeds and brush and there was a yellow and black sign that said: "Protected Area." It didn't seem like many people knew of the spot, but occasionally we'd see a car start to pull up, then back away. Johnny looked over at me, and I could see that his brows were furrowed. I was confused because when we spoke he seemed so mellow and genuinely happy to see me. He was talking on his cell phone and looked pissed off.

I contemplated just driving away. Instead, I rolled down the windows, shut off the engine, and listened to the reeds blowing and some geese squawking in the distance, which made me feel calm and reminded me what I loved about being here. If I told Johnny what happened and apologized maybe he'd see that we'd both gotten past that time when we were together. I was different now. Even though I could have gone away with Val, gotten lost in Thailand, paid for a new identity, and started over, I had done alright for myself in New Orleans. Yet, I couldn't help thinking of how I could have handled Darcy's case differently so things didn't get so messed up.

Johnny looked over and raised his hand while mouthing "five minutes." I didn't have a lot of time, but there probably wouldn't be another chance to talk to him once I headed back to New Orleans. Once I got back, Bruce was going to pounce on me and insist I just get through my caseload, but there was no way I was going to let Darcy's case die, even if I had to do it on my own time. Ever since a bunch of older ADAs quit to go with some of the big firms in town, the caseload seemed insurmountable, and the crime and murder rate was out of control. Darcy had told me that at Nick's Bar, in addition to the aptly named drinks like Kermit's Middle Leg and the 1-800-Fuck-Me-Up, there was a murder pool to guess how many murders New Orleans was going to have that year. When I drove over to Nick's to see what Darcy was talking about, I was scared to get out of my car. Next door there was a rundown motel with hookers hanging around and on the other side, a vacant house all boarded up. The bustling McDonald's around the corner seemed out of place in the middle of blight. But once inside Nick's, I could see what one might see there: a decent jukebox, a crappy pool table, and a couple of cute young bartenders.

My phone vibrated in my bag. I dug down deep and pulled it out, but missed the call. It was a New Orleans phone number, but I didn't recognize it. The car door opened and Johnny slid into the passenger's seat of my car. He put his hands through my hair and kissed me hard, but gently at the same time.

"Johnny..." I started, but he pulled me close and kissed me again. I put my hands on his chest and could feel how strong he'd become.

"I know we don't have a lot of time." His words trailed off as he started to undo my pants. It felt so high school to have sex in a car, but I didn't care. My phone started vibrating again. I ignored it and started to undo Johnny's belt.

"Hang on a sec; I've got to get that." He wasn't fazed and continued taking off my pants. "Hello?" I hesitated.

"Is this Abby?" The voice was a woman's, but young. I didn't recognize it. "She told me to call you in case of emergency," the voice said rapidly, almost like she was getting out of breath.

I sat up and pushed Johnny aside and started to pull my pants back up. "This is Abby. Who told you to call me? Who is this?" Johnny tried to stop my hand but I pushed him away. I could feel my heart start palpitating again. I put my hand over the receiver and whispered, "Can you walk outside for a minute. I can't focus and I've got to take this." I put my hand on his face, rubbing it gently across his stubble. He kissed me softly at the bottom of my neck, then buckled his pants and went outside.

"I'm a friend of Darcy. I can't find her and she's not answering her phone, not at her apartment. We always meet for coffee at PJ's on Maple and she didn't show up, and she always shows up or calls if she can't make it, which is like *never*...."

"Slow down, okay? How many days has this been? I saw her the day before yesterday so she can't have been gone very long. You sure she's not avoiding you or taking a little time for herself?"

"She never does that, never messes up without telling me." The voice was starting to cry, and I realized I hadn't even gotten her name. "And last week at work, I told her she was being a drama queen when she gave me your number. But she was worried, really worried about that guy, especially after all that stuff with the judge. She was convinced someone had been following her."

"Okay, let's stay calm, and tell me everything you can remember. Give me your name and contact info so we can stay in touch." I looked in the rearview mirror and saw Jason's police car drive up behind us. "Shit," I thought. Jason jumped out of the car and screamed something at Johnny, who was closer to the water down by the reeds.

"I'm Nola. I worked with her at the club," she said.

"What club?" I only remembered Darcy telling me about some accounting job she had to make a few extra bucks.

"Didn't she tell you she worked at the Maiden Voyage? She doesn't dance, just works in the office. She always said she wanted to one day, but she was too scared. That's how she met that guy."

"Describe everything you can remember about the last time you saw her and the last conversation you had," I said, trying not to sound too surprised at what she had told me. I never suspected that Darcy would hide anything from me. I saw the guys start yelling at each other, but decided I needed to hear what this girl had to say.

"Well, um, the last time was at F&M's." Nola paused when she said this.

"That was a long time ago before..." she stopped me.

"We went again after the trial, she told me she didn't want to seem scared or anything. She said no one would tell her where she could or couldn't go! I tried to get her to go to another place, but it was like she wanted to prove something."

"You're kidding, right?" I took some notes on some napkins with a pen I'd found in the console.

"He was there that night," she started to talk faster, "but he didn't come up to her or anything. I saw him, he was laughing with a bunch of his fraternity buddies. She didn't drink at all that night, except for the one we had before we left her place. But at the bar, she held on to one of those plastic tumblers and drank soda water. I told her we should leave and go somewhere else, but she wanted to prove something. She said she wasn't leaving first."

"He didn't come up to her later? Maybe you weren't watching? Did she go to the bathroom or anything?"

"We left together. She said she was tired and wanted to go home. I asked if she was sure she didn't want to go over to Maple Leaf or something. She said she wanted to start fresh tomorrow. I dropped her off at her house, and that's the last time I saw her."

"Are you sure she didn't have plans to go anywhere, visit her mom or something?" I wondered if she was depressed about what had happened with the case and that I had let her down. "Listen, Nola, I'm glad you called. But let's not freak out yet, okay? Why don't you go over to her house and knock on the door?"

"That's what I'm trying to tell you! I did! Do you think I'd be calling some stranger lawyer person if I didn't think it was necessary? I called the cops but they don't seem to want to do anything. I didn't know what else to do. Darcy told me how you had helped her. She trusted you and told me I could too."

Johnny came up to my passenger door at that moment, and I held up my hand and mouthed "five minutes." He knocked harder, and I gave him a hard look. He turned away and headed back to his car. "Nola, I'm not in New Orleans right now, so I'm going to have to call a few people. I'll do everything I can to help, I promise. Let's hope that she turns up. You call me as soon as that happens, okay?" I hoped that someone down in the NOPD would take me seriously and do something.

"I'll call a few people she knows and will drive to a few places. You're right, maybe we don't have to freak out yet."

"Call me back in two hours, and we'll take it from there. She's gonna be okay, Nola, I just know it."

"I sure hope you're right, Abby."

"Me too," I said and hung up. I got out of the car and walked over to Johnny, who was standing at the edge of the reeds in a little opening that led to the pond. He heard my door slam and turned around. I walked over to him, reached out, and gave him a hug. He held me, but not as warmly as I might have hoped.

"What were you and Jason fighting about?"

"I honestly can't believe you were with him again after all he's done to us." He took his arms down and stepped back from me. "It's never going to be the same around here for me, is it?"

"It's not what it looks like. I don't know what he told you…."

"I know, I know." He shook his head.

"You're going to kill me for doing this but I have to go. That call was kind of intense. I was working a case for a girl, who is now missing. Her friend called and I'm worried about her. And then of course I have the family waiting…but I'm really glad I got to see you for a little bit." I watched Johnny smile at me in that crooked way that showed his huge dimple under his chin. He knew he made me ramble.

"Heck, I don't care about you being worried about some gal that you obviously care about, no. But becoming engaged to Jason, absolutely."

"You don't seriously believe that?"

"Well, you were stupid enough to sleep with him again, not that it's not really any of my business, is it?" he said, as he stroked my hair and then pulled on my ponytail.

"I'd still like to talk to you again before I leave," I said.

"That would be cool. Give me a shout," he said, and I put my hand right on his heart. "Well?" He put his hand on my shoulder and then kissed my forehead. I looked up and he put his hands behind my neck and pulled me into him; I opened my mouth and pulled him even closer. I could feel his whole body against me.

"I'll call you later," I said. "I have to get back."

As I watched him walk away, get into his truck and drive away, I looked in my rearview and waved. But Johnny didn't see. He was already halfway down the road with a cloud of dust kicking up from his tires.

I decided to stay for a minute. I liked how quiet it was and how I could hear the wind swirling about and geese squawking in the distance. I pulled off the elastic from my ponytail, shaking my hair in my hands, then pulling it back again. I took a deep breath and looked up into the sky at the clouds. The clouds were fluffy and I played an old childhood game I used to play with my dad; I found a dog, a hippo, and even a car. As tears rolled down my face, I laughed to myself at the stupid game we'd played on the back porch during the summer evenings before it was time for him to start grilling the burgers for Corrine and me, and the steak for Mom and him. My eyes were welling up, and the shapes were starting to blur together.

I wanted to call Bruce to see if he could do anything, but it was late. I also thought he'd berate me for having lost control of my case. I dialed Jill and left her a message to do a drive-by at Darcy's apartment and to call me as soon as she did. I hoped to God Darcy had turned up and my worry was for naught. I started my car and backed down the dirt road, wondering if Mom would finally move away and this would be the last time I'd come home.

CHAPTER 8

D riving back to the house, I felt a dull ache in my stomach. As much as I hoped a drive-by from Jill would ease my mind, I couldn't help wondering if this all could have been avoided if I'd called Darcy back. I drove to the library so I could use their computer and get the numbers to call in New Orleans since I'd forgotten to bring my laptop. It was also an excuse for a little bit of privacy. I racked my brain—thinking about bars and hangout places Darcy might have gone. I hoped Nola would know better than I did.

I wondered if Val would be able to find me if I'd gone missing. Sometimes, I felt like she was the grounded one, and I was the flake. I remember when I was trying to decide if I wanted to go to law school or not. She'd said just give yourself permission not to go, and then see how you feel. If Val hadn't harassed me about deciding what I really wanted to do, I might still be waitressing in town or worse, maybe married to Jason with a rug rat or two.

As I got near the library, on my way through the village, the big old elm trees had formed a bridge over the street, like a cocoon. I remembered when they were smaller and the yellow town truck spent days watering them. It didn't seem like they were ever going to get bigger, but that was almost twenty years ago, and so many things had changed. I always hated when the leaves fell because the leaf piles seemed messy. Everything looked so barren and cold—winter was coming.

Just beyond the elms at the junction to the library turnoff, I recognized Charlie's big blue rust-mobile of a truck pass by me with his long surf-casting poles hanging out of the bed, which meant there must be tons of bluefish schools jumping from the shore. If there weren't, he wouldn't waste his time, which is what he had told me earlier at the wake. I had wanted to talk to him a bit more but he seemed so distraught. Soon after I saw him, he left. Since he was the last one to have seen my dad, Charlie might have known if my dad truly had suicidal thoughts. Jason would tell me that guys don't talk about that kind of stuff, but I wondered if Dad confided in Charlie. I couldn't stop thinking about what Corrine said about how jumping off the bridge wouldn't kill someone.

I found a parking spot right in front of the library so I could text without getting into an accident. Then I needed to race home because I couldn't be sure Corrine was checking on anything but herself and a glass of red wine. My cell phone rang just as I was pulling up my email. I answered, "This is Abby," out of habit.

"Is this Abby Callahan?"

"This is," I said.

"This is Jimmy Gautier of the New Orleans Police Department. There's been an accident, Miss Callahan. A young woman has been involved and the only identification she has on her was your number on a slip of paper."

"Oh, God! Is she alive?"

"We can't give out that information over the phone, Miss."

"Please, call me Abby. I work at the DA's office, can you please give me professional courtesy here, Officer Gautier. I'm out of town now and won't be able to get back for a few days."

"You need to come down here and identify the body."

I gasped and said, "I can't get there right now. Is there anyone else that can help? I'm a time zone and a plane ride away. Her name is Darcy, Darcy Smith, and I think her mother lives in St. Louis, but I'm not sure how to contact her."

"Miss, without any identification, the only thing we know is that she had your number on a slip of paper, which is why we need to get you here immediately to identify the body."

"I'm so sorry, I'm at my father's funeral, and I won't be able to leave for another day or two. I can give you the number of a friend of hers in New Orleans and maybe that will help." As much as I tried not to cry, a tear fell down my cheek. The thought of Darcy dead was too much to handle and I felt responsible. I dug into my bag and recited Nola's number from the scrap of paper she'd given me.

"Sorry for your loss, Miss Callahan, and thank you for your help. We're still going to need you to come down to the station as soon as you get back."

"I'll come straight away," I said.

After I hung up, I felt paralyzed to do anything. I gulped at the air, hyperventilating—I forced myself to breathe in through my nose and out my mouth so I could control it. My controlled breathing got me calm again. I hoped that Jill would call and tell me that she found Darcy at her house when she drove by. Then I could call the officer back and tell him I was wrong. I called Nola and told her to call me back immediately because it might be better news coming from me than the cold policeman. I tried to convince myself that it wasn't Darcy. Maybe someone else had written a number down wrong and the whole thing was a big mistake.

I texted Jill to see if she could utilize some of her contacts to find out more information for me. Then I texted Val just four words: Dad died, call me! If that didn't get her attention, nothing would. I started the car up again so I could get home and change for the funeral.

CHAPTER 9

The funeral had gone smoothly, as if there were a script we had followed to the tee, including what turned into a lovely potluck luncheon at the house. Everyone we knew and some we didn't had brought things to share, which I found to be such a heartfelt tribute. It felt quiet now, with Mom and the kids upstairs taking a nap, James in the other room on a business call, and Corrine and I splayed out on the old flower print couches in the living room.

"I have to go upstairs and pack," I said.

"I thought you were staying for a few days?" Corrine yawned as she said this.

"I wish I could stay, but it's that big case I've been working on. I got this crazy call to identify a body at the morgue. I'm praying that they made a mistake and it isn't the girl I've been trying to help."

Corrine sat up and looked at me. "Are you serious?"

"Amazingly, yes. I can't even believe what's happened. I need to go back as soon as I can; I wouldn't feel right if I didn't."

"Don't you think you need to let the police take care of this?"

"I know the timing isn't great, but I feel responsible. I need to go down there and do what they asked, then yes, I'll let them take care of things."

"Guess you gotta do what you gotta do then," she said and

walked back into the kitchen. I thought I heard her say "martyr" under her breath but didn't want to jump into an argument.

I called Jill to let her know, but her phone went immediately to voicemail and said her mailbox was full. I hope this wasn't one of those times she decided to start riding her bike and not talking on her phone. She drove me crazy when she did that because it just meant that she wanted me to drive when we went out drinking. I went upstairs to pack up my stuff.

"Abby, we're going to head out in a little bit to get some dinner," Mom yelled.

I couldn't imagine eating anything else right now, but I said, "Be right down!" I threw on my only pair of jeans and kept Corrine's sweater on. The softness of the cashmere felt so cozy and warm, especially with the damp air. I wondered if maybe she'd let me keep it. Even though I'd gotten used to taking a cool shower, then sweating, as soon as I stepped outside, air-conditioning made me freeze. Someone once told me that New Orleans was the northernmost Caribbean city; on many sweltering summer days, it sure felt like that—the dead-cat stink that sometimes penetrated the sticky air, overpowering the sweet aroma of the magnolias.

Before I went downstairs I took one last look through the flowered drapery that still hung on the windows since I'd had the room. I could see Corrine in the backyard talking on her cellphone, pushing one of the kids on the swings. I loved seeing our faded handprints in the cement around the base of the poles. The swings creaked loudly when anyone got a little too high and that added to the thrill. Mom kept threatening to take it to the dump, but I know Dad wouldn't let her. I remembered Corrine and I having contests to see who could swing the highest. Then we'd take the hose and wet down the slide to see who could slide down the fastest into the kiddie pool we'd set up at the base. Later, when we were in high school, we'd sit out on the swings and talk about boys.

James drove the whole family to the local pub in the grandiose SUV my sister had insisted on buying after the kids started walking. I could remember her yelling, "I'm not a minivan type of person! Could you ever see me driving a minivan?" James never argued; he just got her what she wanted without question. I would have thought that with all the food around us we wouldn't be able to eat another bite, but apparently with Mom crashed out and Corrine so busy chatting with people, neither of them had taken a bite. Once I looked at the menu, my stomach rumbled too. I looked at the menu for a long time, hardly focused on the conversation rumbling around me. Mom was chatting away with Corrine, while Corrine was distracted with getting the kids to pick something and sit still. Corrine's husband James—or Jamie, as she likes to call him—was not only entertaining the kids with coloring books but ordering for everyone.

"How about a salad with chicken, Abby?" He said it so assuredly that I nodded in agreement. It was a relief to just coast through the evening. He was a good guy and as much as I'd love to say that my bitchy sister didn't deserve him, she did. No matter how bad things got, she was hard to hate, because she'd surprise me. Once she handed me two thousand dollars when I had to study for the bar and was completely broke. She refused to let me pay her back until I had a slush fund and then—even then—she would only take four installments of five hundred dollars over the course of a year, so I'd have a reserve for the next time I got into a jam.

"Right, Abby?" Corrine said, but I hadn't heard a lick of the conversation.

"What did you say? Sorry, I missed that."

"Jesus, ignore her. She's in her own world." Corrine motioned for the waiter. "We need some rolls over here and my kids need their orange juices with straws. Thank you very much."

I watched as the waiter scrambled. I wondered if Corrinne had learned this from one of her Southern belle college roommates, because she certainly hadn't learned it here.

"Isn't that Jason?" James said as casually as he could have said, "Pass the ketchup."

I looked up and saw him walking toward the table. I scrambled to stand to meet him halfway when Corrine said, "Hey Jason, great to see you. I think Abby has something for you out in the car."

He looked at me with his head half-cocked, and I said, "Yeah, I do, let's go outside." I gave him a minute to give my mom a hug. He turned toward Corrine, who directed him toward the door.

"So sorry, everyone. Good to see you all." Jason waved and then turned to follow me. The waiter appeared with the orange juice and straws, along with some sourdough rolls, which seemed to distract everyone away from me.

"Jason, say hello to your mother," Mom said, reaching for a roll.

"I will, Mrs. Callahan." I had grabbed his hand and was pulling him away from the table so we could go outside to the parking lot.

Just as we stepped through the dark oak double doors, I said, "Listen, after this afternoon, I don't want to talk to you."

"Hear me out a sec, okay, Abs?" I hated when he called me that.

"There's nothing left to say. You have your car back so can't you just…"

"Johnny, well, you need to stay away from him. Consider this my warning."

"Why couldn't you just have called me to say that? You didn't need to track me down," I said. "And besides, I'm headed back to New Orleans tomorrow so the two of you can just work things out around here."

"Jeez, Abby, I have a girlfriend, you idiot." He reached for me and I pulled away. Then he grabbed my head, leaned into me so I could feel his whole body. I tried to push him away, but he kissed me, and I couldn't help but kiss him back. He stopped abruptly and said, "You got a ride to the airport tomorrow?"

"I'm gonna have Jamie drop me off. He's heading back into the city."

"It's been a tough few days...." Jason kicked a bunch of the blue driveway stones in the parking lot. "Try to hold it together, Abby."

"You know, I am sorry about how everything got so screwed up." I headed back inside before he could answer. Part of me wished I'd shared all the shit that had been going on back in New Orleans because I knew he'd have some interesting perspective, but it was hard enough keeping myself away from him without involving him in my life. I didn't need to give him another reason for keeping whatever we had alive.

I walked back in the restaurant and recognized a lot of faces this time, but I averted my eyes and walked directly over to our table.

"You okay?" my sister whispered to me as I sat down in my chair and put my napkin back on my lap.

"He's such an asshole. Did you know he has a girlfriend?" I started picking at my salad. There was too much dressing on it, but since everyone was almost finished I didn't want to send it back.

"Why do you care? I thought you were over him. And hello, you can't really be surprised that he's still an asshole. I think he might even be engaged to that girl."

"I am over him. It's just when I got here we slept together. It was stupid, I know." I felt both guilty and disgusted that he might be engaged. I didn't want to be that girl.

"Well, you need to move on. Not worth it." She touched my arm, and then quickly went back to eating her salad.

I nodded and watched Corrine's kids and my mom trying to make a French fry design on the table, which normally would have incensed Corrine, but instead, she joined in with ketchup. The waiter brought the kids two bowls of ice cream. I said, "Two more please." Corrine smiled and stuck her tongue out at me.

"I told Jason you guys were going to give me a ride to the airport tomorrow—that okay?"

"Jamie should be able to take you when he heads in. Won't you, sweetie?"

"Sure, I can head in early and prep for my meetings. Abby, what time is your flight?"

"I think it's around 8:30, but if it's too inconvenient I can take a train or something?" I knew James would say yes, because that's the kind of guy he is, but I didn't want to assume.

"We'll be fine. I'll drop you off. Don't worry about it."

"Come on, everyone, no more lollygagging." Corrine started gathering up the kids and her bags. "We've got to get going so Aunt Abby can pack up her things."

"Abby, you're not leaving tomorrow, are you?" Mom sounded so maudlin that I was afraid she was going to break down again.

"I'm sorry, Mom. Remember that big case I was telling you and Dad about? The star witness is missing and the cops need me to identify a body at the morgue. I'm a bit freaked out, but I have to go and see what I can do."

"Can't the police handle this?"

"I asked if someone else could do it, but they said they need me to come back there." I grabbed the crayons and coloring books that the kids had left on the table. James had paid the bill and was already out the door, heading to the car with the kids.

"Is there anything I can do to help?" Mom asked.

"I don't even know what I can do except get back, but thanks."

"Your dad would be really proud of you, Abby." Mom put her hand on my shoulder and looked away so not to cry again.

"I know, Mom, I know." I put my arms around her and hugged her, feeling the bones of her shoulder blades, which made me worry more about her health. As we stepped out the door, I stopped short and thought I saw the same red truck Johnny was driving parked behind the deli next to the restaurant, almost in the same spot as Jason's.

"Come on, let's get a move on!" Corrine pushed me and I followed her out.

Our car was just past the truck, so I had no choice but to walk by. No one was in the driver's seat. I looked around, wondering where he could be—or how he could have found me, but then thought maybe I was being crazy.

"Abby, you're the one who has to get up early tomorrow—get in the car," Mom sputtered. "Come on dear...get in before the kiddos get going again." Out of the corner of my eye, I thought I saw something move.

"Jesus, get a waft of that?" James asked.

I smelled the marijuana, too, and thought, "Yes, he must be nearby." I hoped he had heard me and that somehow, we'd have a real chance to say goodbye, but I wasn't sure. I walked toward where I thought I saw his truck.

"Abby, come on. You're holding everyone up!" Corrine opened the door and stood with her left arm on her hip.

"Can you just give me a..."

Corrine grabbed my arm while I struggled. I turned around and shoved her hard, knocking her to the ground. "Oh, shit, I'm sorry. I didn't mean it." I didn't and Corrine hadn't done anything, but I was so frustrated about everything and couldn't help but take it out on her.

"What's your fucking problem?"

"I'm sorry, Corrine." I put my hand out to help her up, but she pushed it away.

"Just get in the fucking car!" Corrine grunted, standing up and brushing off her pants.

"It's been a long few days." James said. "Can you guys give it a rest?"

At that moment, the truck that had been sitting by the curb tore out of the far side of the parking lot. Without my glasses, I couldn't tell if it was Johnny. "I'm sorry, Corrine, I'm a bitch. I don't know what came over me."

She turned away. "Watch your language. Kids." James put his hand out as if to tell me to stand down, then gave me a nod like everything was going to be okay.

The car full of silence didn't bother me as much as not knowing if Johnny was trying to reach me. When we arrived home, Charlie and his rusty old truck were parked right out front of the house. Maybe his stupid jokes would be just what we needed after a sullen end to what could have been a nice family bonding experience. When we walked up to the front porch where Charlie was sitting, I nearly made an inappropriate sarcastic remark because he also looked like hell—as if he hadn't slept since Dad died. He was bleary-eyed and teary as if he had either been drinking or had just stopped crying.

"We should have asked him to come along," Mom said to Corrine.

"Mom, he didn't even have the decency to show up at the house afterward." Corrine was still snippy even though I'd apologized on the ride home.

"Did it ever occur to you that he might be too upset?" I wasn't looking to start another fight, but I knew Charlie would be devastated about Dad.

"It's a goddamned funeral. We're all upset!" Corrine stormed back to the car to help James with the kids.

I walked up to Charlie and gave him a hug. He smelled like a mixture of Ivory soap and the sea, but not alcohol.

"Abby it's all my fault, I'm sorry…." He started to choke up again.

"Nothing is your fault, Charlie. There was nothing you could have done." I sat down next to him.

"I killed him, and you need to have me arrested." I stepped back and looked at him; I didn't know what to say.

CHAPTER 10

C harlie babbled almost incoherently until we finally got him to sit down at the kitchen table with a hot cup of coffee. Then he pointed to the fridge for a beer.

"There are times when you tell a secret to save someone's life and if it isn't done, you've killed him."

"Charlie, my dear, I can't blame you for honoring him, you wouldn't have been his friend otherwise. If I forgive you, then you must forgive yourself," Mom said and took a sip of red wine.

"She's right, Charlie," I said. "You couldn't have told anyone; you would have lost a friend either way." As I said this, Mom put her hand on Charlie's shoulder and squeezed.

"But you don't understand," he continued. "I thought I had convinced him it was a ridiculous idea, but he said jumping off the bridge won't kill me, just watch." And then he explained how Dad ran around like a little kid and hurled himself off the side of the bridge as he had always wanted to do, but he hit his head by jumping too close. "Stupid! It was such a stupid idea! I'm so sorry. I wanted to stop him, but I was laughing so hard, and then he hit his head. I hope you'll forgive me for not stopping it."

"Seriously, that's what happened?" Corrine started to laugh that low huffy laugh that was a mix of funny, pissed off, and sad. "I knew it, I knew no one could have reasonably offed themselves on that stupid bridge. I can't believe we thought for a minute it was true."

"Well, maybe it's better this way. I mean, he was going to die anyway. At least he was having some fun, wasn't he, Charlie? Both of you are idiots." Charlie tried to smile when Mom said this.

"Charlie, you could have told us and we would have understood. It was horrible thinking that it was suicide, you should have known that," I said, as gently as I could.

Charlie took a swig of the beer still in front of him. "I felt so horrible I couldn't bring myself to tell you, and I was so distraught for not stopping him. I'd told the ambulance crew what happened, but we were a bit drunk so maybe they didn't take me seriously or maybe I joked that it was suicide—but that was before I knew he was dead. I'm so sorry. I didn't mean to let it get out of hand, but I was overwhelmed. I thought you needed to know the truth."

"You know, Charlie, you might have saved us some trouble, but I guess the outcome is still the same, so it doesn't really matter, does it?" I said, pulling my hair back with the rubber band I kept on my right wrist. "The only thing I'm worried about is his reputation. I don't know if it's better that he killed himself or that he was just stupid and jumped off the bridge like a crazy drunk person. I think you ought to set the record straight. That would make us feel better, and it would clear your conscience." I shook my head to myself and thought that maybe Darcy's disappearance might also end up being some silly hoax, and then everything would go back to normal again. I took the last sip of my beer, grabbed four more from the fridge and put them in the middle of the kitchen table.

Corrine grabbed another beer, clicked off the top and took a long pull. "Everyone here still loves you Charlie, even though you were stupid not to have told us sooner."

"Corrine, give it a rest." Mom looked glassy-eyed.

"It's okay, I deserve it. There's no excuse for not telling you all."

"It's over now. And I have to get upstairs if I want to wake up and get to the airport in the morning."

"Gosh, Abby, I didn't realize you were leaving so soon. I thought you'd stay a while and be with ol' what's his face," Charlie said with a smirk. "You know, he spent a ton of time with your dad, so he must be taking this really hard."

I almost blurted out, "He did?" Neither of them had even mentioned more than a sighting of each other so it felt weird to hear Charlie say that.

"You know, it was just in the past few months that they were spending more time together." Charlie read my mind.

"Oh, that's nice." I looked at Corrine, who cocked her head when I said this.

"Guess that boy was keeping tabs on you, trying to win you back and help you with the big case you were working on."

I did a double take. "Did you hear them talking about one of my cases?"

"Sounded like you were pretty concerned about it—which made your dad concerned. He was really proud of you."

"What's the big deal, Abby?" Corrine said.

"Nothing, I guess." I didn't think I'd told him anything too sensitive. I was always careful about sharing privileged information, but I would have been even more careful had I known he was sharing things with Jason. I guess I could have asked his advice after all since he obviously had the background.

"Well, I hate to break up this party, but Abby and I have an early drive tomorrow morning," James announced and brushed his hand over Corrine's hair and gave her a kiss.

"He's right, I have a long day tomorrow. I need to get back to New Orleans," I said.

"Do you really have to leave so soon?" Mom slurred and I

controlled myself from saying anything. "I was hoping we'd spend a little time together."

"You can always come visit me," I said, giving her a quick hug, "Thanks for everything, Corrine. I'm sorry about everything. Let's talk in a few days, okay?"

"I'm going to be traveling for work, but I'll give you a shout," she said, pulling me in to her then swatting me on the butt.

I went upstairs to pack, throwing all my clothes into my suitcase and sitting on it to make sure it closed. I thought about my interactions with Corrine and wished I'd acted better, more mature. I vowed that Dad's death would not tear us apart, but bring us closer together like we used to be. I set my alarm and passed out in my clothes.

* * *

"Abby, over here!" Corrine had her snorkel gear on and was waddling around like a penguin with her flippers. We'd had a taxi drop us off at Chankanaab National Park, since the couple that ran the B&B we were staying in said we had to go there at least once during our stay in Cozumel. During my last year of law school, Corrine and I went on our first and only vacation together. Corrine was single for the first time in years and had said that we needed to do something together.

"Follow me out and tug on my foot if you get scared. You ready?" I might have been more nervous for Corrine than she was. She could swim but was nervous in the water ever since she fell off Charlie's boat. We'd gotten a bit ahead of her and had to turn around, but she'd gotten scared by a school of fish that brushed up against her. She was frantic until we loaded her back on board. I felt like I could live underwater. However, she'd insisted that we needed to snorkel since we were in one of the best snorkeling spots in the world.

I started out slowly and looked behind me to make sure she was there. The water was so clear and there were tons of multicolored fish. I hoped they'd stay clear of her so she wouldn't panic. The water got deep almost immediately, and about thirty feet down there were a manmade wooden cross and other objects resting on the sandy bottom. There were divers down at the bottom among the plants and fish. There was a raft a few hundred yards out. I yelled and pointed, "Swim to that!" Corrine gave me the okay sign and beckoned me to keep going forward. As soon as we got beyond the shoreline, the water deepened. I got to the floating wood raft, which was painted white, and pulled myself up. Corrine was only a few yards away when she popped up, looked back to the shore, and screamed. She started flailing her arms and swallowing water. I didn't think, just jumped back in, reached for her, and pulled her to the raft.

"Did you see something?" I said, my adrenaline pumping. She shook her head no.

"I can't go back; I can't go back!" She was shaking and coughing up water.

"You're okay, Corrine, don't worry." I helped her take off her mask and snorkel as she sat with her feet and fins over the edge of the raft.

"I don't know if I can do it, you're going to have to get me some help." Her eyes were starting to well up. "I almost drowned."

"We'll rest here for a bit. I'll get you back in."

"I don't want you to leave me, Abby. Shit, I wish James were here. He'd know what to do."

"Who's this guy?" Corrine had been through tons of guys, but no one was exactly quite right nor could they handle her strong personality.

"Abby, I think he's the one," she sniffed.

"Well then, we'd better get you back to shore. When you feel ready, you can float on your back…I'll do all the work and bring you in. You won't have to look at the bottom. I'll be talking to you the whole time."

"I don't know if I can do it." She looked like a scared child when she said this, which was weird for me. I'd always looked up to her because she was the one who had always taken care of me as a kid and watched out for me since I'd graduated from school. She was the one I could always rely on and now it was my turn to help her feel safe.

* * *

Corrine wasn't awake when I left in the morning, but I scribbled a note and left it on the kitchen table for her to find. James and I hardly said a word to each other on the way to the airport. We were both fried and it was early. He turned on the radio to 1010AM, which was soothing in its rhythmic monotone news snippets and the traffic report. I zoned out, thinking about the body, the case and a bit of regret for not telling Johnny the truth.

"Abby, why don't you flip back and forth between 1010 and 880 so we make sure we avoid the most traffic."

I played with the radio and asked, "James, does our family drive you crazy?"

"No comment," James said and laughed. "I don't want to get in the middle of you two, but you both need to talk more. She misses you, Abby. I know she doesn't always show it the right way, but that's the truth."

"Thanks for that, James. I miss her too. Don't know why we always fight. I want to get better at talking to her again." I started to feel like the reason I fought with her was because I was a little envious of her life. She had it easy and so many things seemed to go right for her: the perfect husband, kids, a great job. I hated myself for feeling like this and vowed to try to change or at least not revert to being a child when I saw her. It didn't do either of us any good.

I hopped out once we arrived at my terminal with an hour to spare. I waved to James and walked inside so I could get through check-in and get some coffee.

When we piled off the plane, I half expected to see Jill waiting there for me. Instead, there was just a lone Lucky Dog cart. The smell of a Lucky Dog with sauerkraut this early in the morning might have made me vomit even without a hangover. I did, however, welcome the smell of PJ's coffee and immediately went over to grab myself an iced coffee to take downstairs while I waited for my bag. I called Jill, and once again it went immediately to a voicemail message telling me her mailbox was full. Between my big nap and savoring my favorite iced hazelnut coffee, I was optimistic about the day even without a ride home. My bag came down the carousel and I was outside the airport within fifteen minutes of arriving.

I got in the cab and peeled off my sweater as soon as I began to sweat, which felt good! The traffic on I-10 was minimal and when we hit the St. Charles exit, I said, "Just head up past St. Mary's Street, make a left when you can and then left again on Prytania. I'm between Prytania Street and St. Charles Avenue on St. Mary's." I sunk back in the seat and enjoyed the warm breeze through the window.

As soon as we made the left on St. Mary's, I saw my car parked in the good spot near my apartment. Jill was probably still upstairs sleeping in. I don't think she ever got started before lunch and preferred to live in basically the same crappy apartment she lived in while at Tulane, right off Maple Street, which is why she liked staying at my apartment if I was away. My apartment wasn't anything special, but it was a true one-bedroom with high ceilings and beautifully finished amber wood floors, along with a fireplace mantel in the living room and eating nook off the kitchen.

"You need help with your bag, Miss?" the driver said as he double-parked in front of my building.

"That's alright, I've got it." I handed him the money and slid out of the seat. It felt good to be back, and I was looking forward to seeing Jill. She might be able to go with me to the morgue and help me figure out what happened to Darcy.

While the driver was getting my bag out of the trunk, I was trying to find my keys. When I looked up, I saw two men wearing dark suits and dark glasses come rushing out of the building. They trotted over to a black town car that I could see was idling up the street. With only four apartments in the building, I didn't know the goings-on of everyone, but I was sure I'd never seen those men before. I wondered if someone was getting evicted. I'd had beers with the owner, who was about five years older than me and owned a few properties. The other people in the building were a fortyish woman who was the bartender at Molly's in the Quarter, a young guy who lived in the attic apartment and worked for Teach for America, and another guy who I had never seen and could have been one of those men, but he seemed too upscale to live here.

I headed upstairs to my apartment and the door was ajar. I pushed the door open gently; my apartment wasn't trashed and I thought Jill might have just forgotten to lock the door. "Jill?" I called, stepping inside and locking the door. "It's Abby. You up?" The shower was running, so I went to the door and opened it a crack, "Hey Jill, it's me, I'm home!" I looked down, water flowing over the side of the shower. "Jill?" I pushed the door open all the way and saw her lying in the tub with blood on her head and the water splashing over her and onto the floor. "Oh, my God, Jill!" I turned off the water. She was dressed in jeans and a T-shirt and was completely soaked. I slapped her face lightly trying to wake her up. "Jill, wake up, please. It's Abby. Please wake up...." I pulled out my phone and dialed 911.

CHAPTER 11

A s I sat in the waiting room of the hospital, I thought about Darcy and how I needed to get to the morgue. I was also worried about Jill and figured those guys rushing out of my building must have been involved. The craziness of all the recent events only added to my exhaustion from the past few days in New York. I wondered if the doctors had called Jill's parents or whether I should. Even though she didn't want them knowing any of her business, a hospital stay was surely an exception.

A doctor came out from two large swinging doors. She looked around and then back at me, and said, "Are you Abby?" My heart skipped a beat. All I could think of was that she was going to tell me she was dead. I held my breath. "She's okay, just a nasty gash on her head from falling in the tub. You can go in and see her, but we're going to keep her overnight for observation. She told me she slipped, but I see bruises that indicate otherwise. I've called the police to take a statement from her, which is what I must do in these situations. Maybe you can help with some of the questions too."

"Thank you, doctor." I stood up, but felt a bit stunned, especially that Jill was being elusive as to what had happened. I thought talking to the police was a great idea.

"She's right over there in the hallway, until we can find a room for her." The doctor pointed past the nurses' station and to the right, then grabbed a clipboard and headed back down towards the emergency room. I walked passed the nurses' station and no one even looked up. I found Jill with her eyes closed and her head bandaged. I thought about letting her sleep, but I wanted her to know I was there.

I had barely touched her arm when she sat up. "Abby, you have to get me out of here! I can't stay, we need to leave…."

"Jill, they want to keep you here overnight in case you have a concussion. Besides, the police are coming up in a little bit so you can explain everything that happened. Maybe they can get those guys that did this to you." I gently pushed her back down on the bed.

"Abby, it's not safe for either of us. There is a bunch of shit going on, but we can't talk about it here." She whispered and I was starting to think she was a little doped up or plain out of her mind. "I'm not crazy, Abby. I can see the way you're looking at me. I'm not going to piss off the guys that did this especially because I'm sure the cops are involved. You did see how those guys leaving the building were dressed, didn't you? Please help me get out of here to my folks' place, and I'll tell you everything I know, I promise."

"This is crazy talk, Jill. Nothing is going to happen to you here—it's a hospital—and those guys looked like thugs, but not cops," I said, hoping to reason with her.

"Jesus, Abby, we don't have a choice. My head is fine, a few stitches, but I'll live. Maybe the scar will make me look like a badass or at least a Harry Potter wannabe."

"You may have a concussion, Jill; you can't take that lightly."

"Abby, I'll be careful and rest, but please help me out of here. I'm begging you," she said and started to slide off the gurney onto the floor with her feet dangling off the side.

"Alright, but you're gonna owe me big-time for this, especially if we get in trouble."

"If we don't get out of here soon we're both going to be in

trouble. The guys that came to your apartment were looking for you, not me!"

"Why the hell were they looking for me? Jill, you're really starting to freak me out."

"You have any clothes in that big bag of yours?" She hopped on the floor with her bare feet and pointed to my big blue travel bag.

"Does this have anything to do with what happened to the judge in court the other day?" I opened my bag for her and handed her a long-sleeve cotton shirt and a clean pair of undies that I always kept handy in case my luggage didn't arrive.

"Let me take that and you go see if you can find my jeans over there somewhere. Push me back so the nurses don't see." I looked over and there was one nurse at the station, but they were engrossed in a conversation with an older gentleman flailing his hand, while his voice escalated.

I pushed the gurney back and the plastic bag with all her wet clothes dropped to the ground. I handed it to Jill, who took out her jeans and shimmied them on, pulling the hospital gown down inside of them and putting my long-sleeve shirt on too. "I'm keeping these scrubs for pajamas." Jill shoved the scrubs into my bag.

"You're really scaring me, Jill, are you sure you want to do this?"

"Abby, I'm not sure if you realize this but your little friend Darcy and this case are huge and some shit is seriously going to hit the fan. Now let's get the hell out of here. I promise I'll tell you everything once we get to my parents, but just so you know, Darcy is safe."

"I'm going to kill you if you're bullshitting me because I actually rushed back here because of a call from the morgue. I have to go identify a body, and I'm petrified that it's Darcy." As I said this, Jill gasped; I caught her as her legs buckled.

"Jesus, I feel wobbly."

"Maybe you should stay.... Oh my God, there are two cops at the nurses' station now." I put her arm over my shoulder to help her walk without falling. "You're going to owe me big-time for this." I put my arm around her so she wouldn't fall. I didn't know what to believe but Jill seemed so freaked out and I trusted her, so went with it.

"Let's go down that way," she said and pointed toward the back part of the corridor.

"Oh, God, they're coming!" I was starting to freak out about being caught springing a patient.

"Stay calm, just act like we are supposed to be here," Jill said more calmly then before, sliding her arm from over my shoulder to gripping under my arm. When we got to the stairwell, I could hear the cops yelling over to the nurses that Jill wasn't there.

I pulled the door open and let Jill go through first. "Keep going," I said. Then, as she grabbed the rail and started to go down, I closed the door behind us as gently as I could.

We only had a little more than one more floor to go when I heard someone come in to the lower stairwell. I thought I recognized the voice of the doctor I'd met earlier. I signaled Jill to get out on the very next floor. We exited, then followed the signs to the elevators and got on. As the doors started to shut, someone reached their hand in to stop it, but it bounced off. I pressed the button to close the door, when normally I would have held it open. Luckily the elevator doors shut, and we made it to the bottom floor, jumped out and made a sharp right. I kept looking behind us, hoping to find any exit to the hospital.

"You've got to leave the car. We can have someone pick it up later," Jill said, once we got outside.

"Jill, this is crazy. Then how are we supposed to get out of here?"

"Abby, you just have to trust me on this. I'm not being paranoid; I'm trying to be prudent. If you'll humor me until we get to my parents, I know you're going to understand. Please, Abby, trust me."

I did trust her, which was the only reason I was going along with this harebrained idea.

A cab swung around the corner as we stepped outside, I flagged him down before he made it to the entrance. Jill stood still with her back up against the building. Once the cab stopped, I jumped in, and she ran over and slid in beside me. "I don't think anyone saw us," she said.

"We're fine. Now, please give him the address," I said.

We hadn't gone but a half a block when Jill yelled, "Down!" and pulled me down in the seat. As we drove by my car, there were two cops circling it on foot. The glass from the driver's side window was shattered all over the ground.

"What the hell is going on? This is getting ridiculous and I'm not going to play along unless you tell me something," I said.

"It's about Darcy," she said and I gulped. I thought for sure she must be dead.

CHAPTER 12

Jill's parents' house was in the French Quarter, about a ten-minute cab ride from the hospital. Once we got near, it took another few minutes to navigate through the one-way streets and narrow pathways between parked cars on both sides of the street.

"Jeez, Abby, I never asked you about the funeral and what happened while you were there. Did you see your ex too?" Jill pointed for the driver to drop us off on the corner.

"It was an absolute shit show and I've mostly been in shock. I saw both of my exes, which was nuts. I can't believe my dad is gone, it doesn't feel real yet," I said, holding the front of the cab seat as the cabbie slammed on the brakes.

"Jesus, man," Jill yelled as we jerked forward. "Over there is good."

"Now that you're okay, I'm going to head over to the morgue. That's why I came back early. They had called me in New York because a woman was found dead with my number in her pocket. I hope to God it's not Darcy."

"Oh, my God! Abby, I definitely need to go with you."

"You need to rest, Jill. I can handle this," I said, even though I probably couldn't, but I needed to, I owed it to Darcy.

"You saw what happened at the hospital. We need to stick together, but it's not Darcy. It can't be."

"Well, that's what I need to find out." I felt determined and like I was wasting time not getting there already.

"Just come inside for a bit. We can get a ride. It'll be easier, and I want to go with you."

"I guess I would feel better going together." The cab parked, and I scrambled to get my purse.

"Do you mind paying? I can get you back later, I have nothing on me." I rolled my eyes, paid the driver, and we hopped out.

The street was quiet, except for a few tourists meandering about. We walked up to a tall, yellow painted wall that seemed like a blockade around a corner property.

"The entrance is down over there, past that magnolia tree. I hope to hell that someone forgot to lock the door today." As she walked, I could hear the swish of Jill's legs from her wet jeans rubbing against each other. We came up to a tall unassuming doorway, and she jiggled the lock. "This thing is a piece of shit." She reached around a broken piece of wood, jiggled a little more and then the door came ajar. "Big-time security, huh?"

"You'd better tell your parents they need to replace that." We stepped in to the courtyard and went around to the left of the fountain towards the guesthouse. I expected one of her family's chocolate labs to come bounding around the corner like they usually did, but it didn't look like anyone was home.

"I've got to get out of these jeans. Then, I can tell you the whole scoop on the way over to the morgue, okay?"

"Start telling me now, Jill—maybe with why the cops were hovering around my car? And why this covert operation of breaking you out of the hospital was necessary?" I needed to know why we were acting like this because it seemed crazy and I didn't want to play games.

"You started something when you refused to back off Darcy's case." She bent down to a flower pot, lifted it up and grabbed the secret key to the house. The former slave quarters, now a guesthouse, was painted the same pale yellow as the house, but the guesthouse was on the opposite side of the courtyard on the far-left corner of the property.

"I don't understand. She was found in a park, raped and beaten. If anything, Chip started something when he raped her. Not my fault his father is a bigwig! I refuse to be intimidated by someone like that."

"See, Abby, that is exactly the problem. You just wouldn't let this one go," Jill said and opened the door to the cottage. I followed her upstairs. There were two small bedrooms upstairs, with color coordinated flowered bedspreads in one room and mixed color stripes in the other, with big antique dressers dominating both rooms. Jill dug into the bottom of her dresser and pulled out a black cotton skirt and top. "Can you give these a pull for me?" She sat down on the bed. I pulled on her jeans and fell backwards into the wall, which shook a little. She laughed. "This is not the sturdiest structure."

"Now tell me what the hell happened to you at my apartment and why some thugs would be looking for me." I got up and sat down next to her, crossing my arms. I wasn't going to let her off the hook without an explanation. I hadn't even been home for a few hours and already I was thrust into a drama.

"Those two guys were off-duty cops looking for Darcy. They didn't believe me when I told them you weren't home and I didn't know who Darcy was."

"This must be connected to that judge getting arrested or Chip. But I can't believe they came to my place looking for her. I told the cops that she might be the girl at the morgue. I'm so sorry that you took the brunt of this. You could have been killed."

I told Jill about Nola calling me, telling me that Darcy was missing, which made me race back when I really needed more time with my family, when she blurted, "Nola, Nola called you?" I looked at her, dumbfounded.

"How do you know about Nola? What exactly is going on around here?" I leaned forward and put my feet on the ground. Jill had her back to me and was pulling on her skirt, which looked funny on her since she often wore jeans no matter how hot it was. She threw on a t-shirt from one of the drawers. Then, she grabbed my wrist, pulled off my hair band from it, and swooped up her long blond hair into a ponytail, adjusting the gauze around her head so it looked like a headband.

"Nola and Darcy worked in one of those gentleman's clubs down here in the Quarter. I've been doing a little research myself and found out that your innocent little victim was not really so innocent."

"What? When'd you start doing your own investigation? And why the hell didn't you call me when you found this shit out?" I was flabbergasted and pissed. "What the hell, Jill, why are you holding out on me when you know I could use this information for my case?"

"I couldn't tell you anything until I had my facts in order. Also, I didn't want to contaminate your case when you were so intent on doing the right thing for that girl."

"You could have saved me a lot of agony. How long have you been working on this?" I walked across the room and got a glimpse of myself in the mirror and saw that my ponytail was unkempt.

Jill sat on the bed next to me and put her arm around my shoulder. "Jesus, Abby, don't you think I wanted you to win that case too? I wasn't thinking about you as much as I was that this case was spicy and I wanted to do my own recon, get a scoop, then maybe help you out too."

"Jeez, Jill...." I took my ponytail out, pulled my hair back, and ran my hands through my scalp a few times before putting my hair back into another ponytail. "Tell me exactly what you found out in this so called recon mission, which is honestly making me feel like I didn't do a very good job here. Maybe I was just too distracted with everything going on." I moved to the middle of the bed and she turned around to face me.

"Abby, what I found out is nothing that you could have known. People lied, yes, including Darcy, so you knew everything you were meant to know. I think you really had a good shot there until the situation with the judge."

"Yes, but it's my job to be prepared for my case and I should have been able to get every bit of information I needed over the course of two months!"

"Abby, the cops are supposed to get you the information, so don't beat yourself up about this. You did the best you could do under the circumstances. Are you okay? I mean, with your dad and stuff. I would be a complete basket case."

"Well, anything could make me cry right now, but I'm really focused on making sure Darcy is safe. How are you feeling—let me see your head. I think you should probably get in bed for a while."

"I'm fine, Abby, really. I have a little a bit of a headache, but that's it. This is more important anyway."

"You could have a concussion, so if you feel weird or headachy you probably need to get back to the hospital."

"I haven't even gotten to hear the whole story of what happened to your dad. Tell me before we get ahead of ourselves here, I'm sorry."

"You know, it wasn't a suicide, which was a relief of sorts. However, he jumped off a bridge like a freaking teenager if you can believe it, hit his head, and drowned."

Jill gasped. "Seriously? Wow, that is tragic, but kind of cool in a way. I mean, he was dying so maybe it's better he didn't suffer?"

"Part of me is so angry, you know. But another part of me is happy he did something crazy if that's what he wanted to do. I don't think he suffered, so maybe it all worked out for the best." My eyes started to well up.

"Abby, this is all too much for you. Why don't you let me take care of things?"

"Thanks, but you know I can't. All this craziness is certainly keeping my mind occupied on other things for the moment. So, tell me what else happened here while I was gone?"

"Short version is that I got in touch with Val and got Darcy a ticket to Bangkok with instructions to stay with Val until all of this shit dies down."

"Why would you do that, Jill? You must have had to rifle through my stuff to find Val's info, huh?" I got off the bed to get my bag. "I can't even *get in touch* with Val and you manage to not only reach her but also involve her by sending a girl to her that you don't even know?"

"Listen, Abby, you would have wanted me to do this. I mean, with you back in New York taking care of family stuff, you needed me to use all my investigative skills to find out what was really going on. Think about it? You would have asked me to do this if you were here."

"Well, thanks, I guess. But I really wish you would have told me what you were doing."

"Um, I would have, but honestly I thought you'd be in quite a state, and I could have this wrapped up with a bow for you when you got back."

"Sending Darcy to meet up with Val in Thailand sounds a little over the top, don't you think? What's wrong with going to the proper authorities?"

"You saw what happened to the judge, so, honestly, who could I really trust? After you left, I called Two-Poke, you know, my old roommate who always got too drunk and fell asleep on every girl he brought home? He loved those clubs and was kind of a regular. I thought he might even know the girls and it wouldn't take much to get him to do a 'research' project with me. So, I asked him the name of the club he used to go to and if he had heard of a girl named Darcy. He couldn't remember and said they don't use their real names anyhow. So, I thought I'd go down there myself to see if I could find out some more information. I figured if I found anything I'd tell you."

"Jill this is a lot to process, I mean that's kinda crazy, isn't it? I mean it's not like you'd be inconspicuous going into a club like that."

My cellphone rang again, I reached into my bag. It was Jason again—I switched it off. "How did you even know what Darcy looked like?"

"I hung out in the back of the courtroom to cheer you on while you were in the trial. Besides, you talked about her so much over the past few months I felt like I knew her."

"I really wish you had told me what you were up to." I was trying not to be pissed off because I knew she meant well, but part of me felt betrayed.

"Abby, you know Darcy was bullshitting you about being a sweet little college gal with a paperwork job at a French Quarter restaurant, don't you?"

I shook my head. "I believed her and she had the pay stubs to prove it. You know that would have hurt us at trial."

"Are you that naive? I mean, it didn't take me much to find out that Chip's dad was connected to the club."

"What?" I'd gotten so hung up in the case that I'd taken what Darcy said at face value and forgotten to open my eyes and do my job. I couldn't imagine why a successful defense attorney would want to be a part of a club like that. It all seemed very fishy and I had completely missed it.

"You know, there's a lot of money in that kind of club. A lot of people have stakes in them, but they're not always dirty. This one is classy, with a hundred-buck cover to get in, and then of course, you've got to drink. I'm sure there's a table minimum."

"How'd they let you in?"

"Two-Poke was totally game for a secret mission, especially if there was free booze and girls involved. I told him I'd drive and he could get as piss-drunk as he liked and I wouldn't say a word, so long as he got me in. Obviously, I don't look like the type that would frequent one of those places, and I couldn't really say I was a reporter." As Jill said this, she got up and went to the bathroom, continuing to talk while she peed. "I couldn't really tell Chris what's going on, but I did tell him I was looking for a girl named Darcy. I asked him to discreetly find out who Darcy was and whether she was at the club."

"Don't tell me, he tries to help you by buying lap dances?"

"Kind of. I mean this is a classy place. You pick a girl you want to dance with and the hostess arranges it. You can go over to a private area if you want."

"I'm seriously feeling like I got duped because I didn't know all this shit about Darcy. She's a liar, but I should have pressed her harder. I feel responsible for what happened and I'm not going to be able to relax until I know she's okay."

Suddenly, there was a hard knock on the door, making both of us jump up from the bed.

"Anyone in here?" an older woman bellowed in the sweetest of tunes.

"In here Vee!" Jill sang back. Vee was Jill's parents' housekeeper who had been with them about thirty years.

"Jill honey, it's so nice to see you. I thought I saw some commotion over here, and I wanted to make sure I hadn't left things open."

"You remember Abby?" Jill gestured to me and Vee nodded. Then she went over and gave Vee a hug. Vee was about sixty years old, short, and round. She wore a blue-and-white pinafore uniform even though Jill's mom had told her that a uniform wasn't required years ago. She was more like family than a servant. "Vee, can you please let Mom know that I'm going to be staying here for a few days? I'm hiding out from Tucker, who's been skulking around my apartment, and don't want anyone to know I'm here, but I also don't want mom to freak out." Tucker was Jill's ex-boyfriend who had roughed her up a little. She'd had to get an order of protection against him.

"When did you get back together with Tucker?" Vee brushed back Jill's hair from her face and looked under her bandage. "Did he do this to you?"

"No, I'm not with Tucker, but if you say I fell down and needed to rest at home Mom will lay off my back. Please don't mention him, you know how she is. Abby can vouch for me that Tucker didn't do it, can't you Abby? I've been working on a really important story and need to have privacy," Jill said. I was pretty sure Tucker had moved out of town and that part of this was true even though I wasn't sure why Jill wouldn't tell the whole thing to Vee if she trusted her like she said she did.

"Can't I tell her that? If I mention Tucker and she sees your head, she's going to want to call the police."

"You're right, that's a good idea—tell her I'm working on a story."

"Jill, what's going on here?"

"Please, Vee, just tell her…." Jill gave Vee another hug. Vee smiled warmly and winked at me, reminding me of my own grandmother. She was very much like a mother to Jill, who always said, if there was anyone from her family she could trust, it was Vee, which is why I didn't understand why she'd lied. I wished she'd told her the whole story.

"Let me know if you girls need anything." Vee left and headed back across the courtyard to the main house.

Jill then told me how Two-Poke Chris kept on telling her that she was wrecking his mojo until she reminded him that she was paying for the lap dances as part of her research. Finally, a new girl came up to him and started dancing. "Said her name was Nola. He said *Lola*? And she said no, *Nola*, you know, like the nickname for New Orleans, Louisiana. I mean, a name like that is hard to forget, right?"

"Well, it can't be a coincidence that a girl named *Nola* called me, told me she was friends with Darcy and that Darcy was missing!"

"Well, she takes the fifty Chris was holding and presses a note into his hand that simply said, '12AM REAR ENTRANCE ALONE.' I didn't feel great about meeting her like that, made me kind of nervous..."

"You didn't go by yourself, did you Jill?"

"Of course, Mr. Two-*fucking*-Poke got drunk and ended up finding a girl that would go home with him, so I put them both in the back of my car and drove around back. I was relieved when I saw Darcy, whom I recognized immediately because of the trial, pacing back and forth and checking her watch. She was alone, pacing and seemed nervous. I told her I was a friend of yours, and I was trying to help you. She didn't believe me until I told her about your dad and that you had to rush back to New York. She started to cry, gushing about how she'd gotten sucked into this to pay for school and that Chip was trying to get her to do some extra work on the side. She didn't want to and that's when he roughed her up, raped her, and left her in Audubon Park."

"Why didn't she tell me? If I had known this, it could have helped her case."

"She was embarrassed. And she was trying to blackmail Chip and his father, which she didn't want to come out at the trial. If she hadn't ended up at the hospital because of you, she probably would have gone home and nursed her wounds. Instead, she found a zealot—you know there was no stopping you! Besides, if you won—like you said you could—then Chip might go to jail, which may not have helped her, but would have given the other girls a safer environment."

"How do we know that Darcy is in Thailand now with Val? How could you have thought this was okay, Jill? Why didn't you go to the police?" I was so angry at Jill my head was spinning and I felt like I was going to explode. Jill waited and watched me pace around the room for a minute until I finally dead stopped, stared at her, and said, "Say something I can grab onto here."

"Abby, you know I'm on your side. It was the only thing I could think of to keep her safe. We can't trust the cops. Val had been trying to get in touch with you but was having a difficult time getting a connection to a cell phone. When she called your landline, I picked up the phone out of habit. I'm glad I did because I could tell her what was going on with you. It was her idea to help Darcy and, to be honest, it didn't seem like the worst idea."

I started to nod as she said this because even though it was crazy, it was totally something Val might do. But then, I thought if Val knew what happened, she would have tried to get in touch with me. I felt accusatory when I said, "Jill, Val didn't call me while I was in New York; she knows my number. I just don't understand."

"She was having some cell service issues wherever she was. As it was, we were cutting in and out and she ended up calling back a few times. She promised to call once Darcy arrived and when you were in a better space," Jill said and sat down beside me on the bed. She was earnest and apologetic and I knew that Val was a flake, so none of it really surprised me.

I'd told Jill all the crazy stories about losing phones, running out of charge, being in places where it felt like she was on another planet. "I know you don't have any reason to lie to me, but you have to admit this is a lot to take in."

"Abby, I couldn't make this shit up if I tried. Think about it."

"I know, Jill, but this just sounds like the most ridiculous plan I've ever heard. Did you at least get a number for me to call Val?"

"She doesn't have a number; that's why she has to call us."

"I guess we'll have to see what happens then. I still want to go down to the morgue to verify things, even though I know it's not Darcy. I told them I would and I want to do it before they close. I don't want to hold up the notification any more than I already have."

"I want to get to the bottom of this, not only for us, but for Darcy too. I don't know what would have happened if it was you instead of me at your house today." She looked out the window and then moved to open the door again for Vee. "Vee, you just can't help yourself, can you?" She took the sandwiches and a glass of iced tea that Vee held out to her.

"You gals couldn't have had time to get lunch, and I don't get to do this often enough." She chuckled, then coughed.

"You're the best, thank you. I think we could use these."

"Are you ladies going to be back for dinner?"

"I think so. Is Walt around to give us a quick lift? We don't have a car right now."

"Walter is working on something in the garage. I'll see if I can't get him to help you out." Walter was Vee's husband and the handyman of the property who'd been with the family forever.

"Let's eat, and then we'll go over to the morgue. I don't feel comfortable getting your car yet, and it will be easier if Walter waits for us."

My cellphone rang again. I answered it and said, "Jason, what's going on?"

"Abby, you need to...Johnny..." The reception was spotty but his voice sounded annoyed.

"I don't know what you're doing, but please don't call me!" I yelled into the phone, as if he was hard of hearing.

"He's starting to ask questions, and it's going to come back to us." The clarity in the sound and what Jason said hit me hard and hit me in the gut.

"It was a long time ago; it doesn't matter anymore." Of course, it *did* matter to me, but if I kept telling myself it didn't, maybe I could stop feeling so guilty.

"It matters to him, Abby...." Jason's last words trailed off. I hung up the phone. I didn't believe him, but it didn't matter because it wasn't my fault. I'd kept silent, but it was too late to undo things now.

* * *

I thought back to the accident. I was so drunk the whole thing felt like a nightmare that I couldn't wake up from. I stumbled from the car and fell, only coming to when Jason must have arrived and shook me. He'd been following us because he suspected that we were fooling around. I was sitting on the curb, away from the accident with my head in my hands bawling; I'd never felt so sorry in my life. Jason staged the accident—moving Johnny to the driver's side. He did it so easily and I gawked, not thinking clearly enough to stop him, and when I tried to speak, he shut me down, telling me that it wasn't going to be a big deal and I needed to shut the hell up. When he was finished, he told me to hold it together and not say a thing while he called it in.

Letting Johnny take the rap for the accident was the most horrible thing I'd ever done and something I never stopped thinking about. Darcy's case made me feel like I could make amends in some way—do something good and noble. I'm not sure why Johnny didn't fight it, and why I was never called as a witness. So many of the details were fuzzy. Was it possible that it didn't really happen the way I thought it did?

* * *

"Do you want to talk to me about what happened with Jason?" Jill looked at me as I grunted and nearly threw my phone.

"There's nothing to tell really except that he was there, and I got to see Johnny, you know, my old flame who just got out of jail. Jason just tries to manipulate me and I can't take it. I want the past to just stay in the past, you know what I mean? I really screwed up everything a long time ago, and he just can't let it go."

"Did you sleep with him when you were home?"

"Ugh, I did. So stupid. He looked hot and it just happened. I probably would have controlled myself if he had told me he had a girlfriend. Now, I feel gross about it."

"Well, there's nothing you can do about it now, is there?" Jill kind of laughed when she said this.

I shook my head. "And then I saw Johnny and we didn't sleep together but I wanted to. How screwed up is that?"

"Was it weird to see Johnny after all that time?"

"Yes and no. Going back there made me realize that it's so much better for me here."

"You always have the memory. And you're such a slut, you know I have to tell you that." Jill shoved me gently when she said this. We had our differences but she was the most loyal friend I had in New Orleans.

CHAPTER 13

I followed Jill over to the main house, where Walter was waiting for us by the car, an a big, old, white Cadillac. Vee had asked him to drive us to the morgue. He hugged Jill warmly, and then gave me a bear hug too.

"Any friend of Jill is a friend of mine," he said.

"Nice to finally meet you, Walter," I said.

He was a bit older than Vee, with a head full of white hair. Jill told me he always wore neatly pressed blue jeans, which was one of the reasons she also wore jeans almost anytime of year, even with the heat and humidity. Walter had taught her the basics of car repair and how to throw a football. She always said you could learn a lot about life from a guy like him.

"Darcy is fine. You sure you still need to go?" Jill lingered before getting in the car.

"It's my responsibility to go no matter what. Besides, I'd never forgive myself if you were wrong. How do I really know if your Thailand scheme is going to work out?"

"I just don't want us to waste time. That's all," Jill said and got into the car.

"You don't need to come, Jill."

"I want to. Maybe it will help give us some answers about what happened at your apartment earlier."

"You know, that's the part that scares me. I mean, I work for the DA's office. I'm on the same side as them!"

Jill turned around to look at me from the front seat of her mom's Cadillac. "Listen, I'm going to need a little more time to figure this all out, but Chip's dad's arm must reach pretty far. If we can expose whatever he's doing over there, the fallout will be huge."

Without taking his eyes of the road, Walter put his hand on Jill's shoulder and said, "Girls, the sound of this is getting me concerned. What is going on with you two?"

"Walter, if we told you the half of it, you wouldn't believe us. But right now, Abby got called back to go identify a body. That's where we need to start."

"Alright, but if you two are in some kind of trouble, you need to let me in on it. Maybe I can help?"

"We're fine, Walter," Jill said and glared at me. She turned down the radio and stared ahead, which was the only time I sensed Jill had a bit of elitism.

Walter turned down the radio and said, "A story is only worth so much, and I don't want to see you get into any trouble now, Jill. Why don't you reach out to my nephew Calvin? He's still working a beat in Jefferson Parish—you know you can trust him. I'll give you his number in case you don't have it."

"You know, Walt, that's a great idea and that he's not in Orleans Parish is perfect," I said.

"We probably shouldn't bother Cal, unless we can't figure things out on our own." Jill was abrupt. "Abby, you'll screw things up by freelancing in another parish."

"They've asked him to teach at the academy. He's done so well for himself."

"Walt, I've seen him, not often, but sometimes we'll be in the same haunts."

"That's real good, Jill. Calvin, he's good people, and your dad did right by him."

Jill looked at me. "You're right, Walt. Why not talk to Cal and get his perspective? It's not like we have to tell him everything but he'll definitely give us good advice."

"But you just said…" It wasn't like Jill to flip-flop so easily. I wondered if she had a history with Cal that she didn't want to tell me about.

"Forget what I said. What harm could it do to have someone else on our side?"

We arrived at the morgue. "I'm going to spin around and find a spot to park. Give me a call when you're done. I'll also give Cal a shout while you're in there. Maybe when he's off duty we can meet up." Walter lifted his cap and wiped the sweat off his brow. Instead of cranking up the AC like most of us did, Walter preferred to keep the windows open with the air on low to make sure he could hear the world.

"You're the best, Walt." Jill gave him a kiss on the cheek before we both hopped out of the car. I patted his shoulder from the back seat as I slid out the side.

I'd been to the morgue a few times, but never to identify someone. I was afraid that we'd be going into a big refrigerated room with large drawers filled with people. I imagined we'd go into that big ice-cold room and they'd pull out the drawer for us to see the body. I hoped that neither of us would pass out. We walked into a reception area, which was nondescript and barren but for the reception desk and a few chairs, and I told the gum-chomping girl behind the desk that I had been called to identify a body.

"Jesus, it's like a morgue in here." Jill poked me in the side with her elbow.

"Not funny." I was nervous and wasn't sure what to expect or what I had to do to identify a body.

"Oh yeah," the woman said in between chomps of her gum. "I need to get a copy of one of your licenses. Go down the hall to Office Number 3, down there on the right. Doctor Mackinaw handles all the missing persons. He should be right back; he's getting a coffee."

I handed her my license and soon she was handing it back and shooing us down the hallway, buzzing us through the big glass doors. Some security system, I thought.

We went down the hall and sat down in the two chairs in front of a desk that was overrun with files. A small pile of pictures sat right in the middle of his desk. On the walls were a bunch of framed degrees from the University of Michigan and Kalamazoo College along with a large, multicolored cubist canvas that was signed in the bottom right corner. I wondered how Doctor Fred Mackinaw ended up working in a morgue in New Orleans. Jill leaned forward to check out the pictures when in walked a thirty-something guy in a white coat, dark-rimmed glasses, and short dark hair in disarray.

"I'm Doctor Mackinaw, I'm the forensic pathologist in charge of identifications. Can you please give me your names?" He sat down and started flipping through the pictures while I told him my name and explained that I'd received a call from the police to make an identification. Before I even finished the sentence, he said, "I've got it," and he put a picture down in front of me. I breathed a sigh of relief: It was another young woman who looked around Darcy's age. Jill, however, had started to hyperventilate.

"What, Jill? Do you know her? Who is that?"

"That's Nola! The girl we spoke to at the club!"

"Oh, my God! She must have had my number on her from when she called to tell me about Darcy. I told her to go to Darcy's apartment!"

I faced Jill: "Calm down, Jill, please, hold it together." Jill pulled it together quickly and took a pad out to take some notes.

"Do you have any other information about this woman?" The doctor, with his pen in his hand, was looking down at his own notes.

"No, nothing at all," Jill said and stood up abruptly. "Come on now, Abby, we have to go."

"Jill, don't you want to…" I started, but Jill pulled my arm.

"Abby, we need to leave now." She started walking down the hallway, dragging me along with the doctor following.

"We're going to have you two talk to the cops and tell them what you know so we can notify this woman's parents," he protested. Now I understood why Jill wanted to get out of there so fast. We could not guarantee that we'd be talking to good cops. We couldn't risk it.

"Maiden Voyage Club!" I yelled just before we got to the door. I didn't want to leave poor Nola's parents with no clue at all and hoped that Doctor Mackinaw would look into things himself. We didn't know anything else about her, except that she was a friend of Darcy. The door clicked but wouldn't open because the gum-chewing receptionist had to buzz us out.

"Girls, please don't leave. Please sit down and tell me what you know. I really don't like a cold case. If you know this girl, then you owe it to her to help us and her family." I turned around; he was right. We owed it to Nola.

"If you don't call the cops right now, we'll stay. But there's something serious going on, and we're afraid for our safety," Jill said commandingly and the doctor looked taken aback. I'd never seen this side of her, but perhaps it was just the stress of the day?

"Listen, my main concern is the identification of the body and personally, I hate when I see someone so young. Your information will help me and the girl's family. It's the right thing to do. The detectives have the same information we do so I'm sure with your number on hand, they'll be contacting you shortly, if they haven't already."

"Oh, God!" I gasped. Now I knew why some cops without uniforms were at my door of my apartment. We told Doctor

Mackinaw enough to answer all his questions so Nola could be properly found. I also told him about my case with Darcy and that Nola had been worried enough to call me. Jill kicked me when I told him but I didn't see the harm.

"I can't tell you how helpful this is—having a little to go on before we go to dental records really makes my life a little easier. Although what you've been saying has gotten me thinking about another case that rolled in, also without ID. It's very similar but this poor girl had one of those messenger bags full of stuff."

"A what?" I started trembling from the inside out.

"You know, one of those bags, kind of like the one you have there. You mind coming back to my office, maybe you can help."

"Please no, please no," I whispered to myself and to Jill, who was walking with her mouth agape and gripping my arm.

CHAPTER 14

S itting in Doctor Mackinaw's office again, I held my breath as he shuffled through a few files until he found what he wanted to show us. I thought back to the first time Darcy and I had a conversation in my office. She talked about how her dad would have come to New Orleans and killed Chip for doing what he had done to her that night. First, he would have lectured her about what she was wearing and going out at night, but then he would have gotten in his car and drove down. He died a few years back, and she missed him terribly. I could relate to her and had thought by talking about my dad that I'd gotten her to trust me. Now I just wondered if she was playing me.

"I'm going to slide this photo over to you, and I hope you'll be able to tell me something. I'm sorry, though…I do hope it's not the friend you're worried about." Doctor Mackinaw pushed the photo over to us.

I grabbed the photo. "I don't know her! I don't know her!" I felt a weird mixture of being elated and feeling guilty at the same time. She was a young girl, seemingly around Darcy's age, but it wasn't her. I wondered if the bag was a coincidence.

Jill looked at the photo in my hand. "Shit, I don't know her either." We both looked at Doctor Mackinaw, who seemed stoic about our revelation. Although you could tell he was used to this, there was a kindness in his eyes, some humanity beyond the science. "Do you think this girl's death is connected to Nola?"

"Well, I shouldn't really be telling you this, but they were both found in Louis Armstrong Park in the past forty-eight hours, so yes, they're related in some way."

"I just got goosebumps." I could tell by the way Jill was tapping her foot that she had more to say, but she was holding back, and I wasn't sure why.

"Even *I* don't go into that park by myself." Doctor Mackinaw put the picture back in a large manila envelope.

"Can we look at that bag to see if it's our friend's? It really looks like it, and maybe it will give you a clue if I can find something." I felt bold asking him, but I hoped he'd just say yes. I was surprised that the cops hadn't taken it for evidence. He pulled the bag up from behind his desk. "Why don't you take a quick look, and tell me if you see anything? I haven't had the time to inventory it yet, so please watch the integrity of what's in it. The cops are coming back to get it in a little bit."

I knew it was Darcy's bag not only because of the color but also because it had a nail polish stain on the front flap. I smiled when I saw she had *A Confederacy of Dunces,* a book I'd told her I'd thrown against the wall because the main character Ignatius J. Reilly was so annoying. "She wouldn't have left this on purpose. And she wouldn't have left the country without it," I whispered to Jill while Doctor Mackinaw had his back turned. I wasn't so sure she'd gotten on that plane to Thailand and thought maybe something else had happened to her. I dug through one of the front pockets and found a matchbook to Deanna's Bar and Grill, which was on Rampart, right by Louis Armstrong Park. I thought about putting it in my pocket, but I flashed it to Jill and put it back. Darcy had once told me I had to go there on the night that Kermit Ruffins played and that we should meet there for some music and "the most amazing red beans and rice." I'd never managed to make it over there, but tonight I intended to find out for myself.

I pushed the bag back to Doctor Mackinaw and Jill said, "Sorry we couldn't be of any more help." I looked over at her, but she stared straight ahead and hit my knee, so I played along.

"Thank you both for helping me. If you have any additional information, call the police or you can call me, and I'll get the info to them. I do hope your friend is okay." He gave one of his cards to each of us. We all stood at the same time. "Judy will buzz you out." He pointed toward the way we came in.

"Thank you, Doctor," we both said in unison. He nodded and headed back down the dark hallway to the reception area.

As soon as we stepped outside the building, I felt a rush of hot air hit me. "You know, Covenant House is over by Louis Armstrong Park. If Darcy was going to hide out somewhere, why not the Catholic homeless shelter? She could be anonymous, and it would be safe for a while. And it's on Rampart…"

"…right by Deanna's," Jill finished my sentence. "But she must be in Thailand by now. I gave her money and specific instructions." Jill spotted Walt and started walking over to him. I followed.

"You didn't buy her the ticket?" I asked.

"We looked online together and bought the ticket. Then I gave her a little money to get by for a bit."

"We need to call the airline and see what we can find out. Better yet, maybe Val will have sent you the confirmation you had asked for. Was she going to call you or email?"

"It wasn't clear, only that she would notify me as soon as Darcy arrived in Bangkok. She was only a few hours away, so she should have been there to meet her at the airport."

"You know, this is one fucked-up plan you concocted." I was still in disbelief, and I wondered if there was something she might not be telling me.

"Listen, if you had seen how terrified she was, you probably would have done the same thing."

"No, Jill, I probably would have gone to the police," I said and crossed my arms.

"Well, now you know *that* would have been a stupid idea."

"No matter what, we need to go there tonight and see if anyone there had a clue about the missing girl or Darcy." The dead girl having Darcy's bag wasn't just a weird coincidence and I knew I had to try to find out what happened. We might be the only ones who could.

"We should call Cal. He'll be able to help us find out what's going on," Jill said, scanning the street again.

"You okay, Jill?"

"Just feeling a bit jumpy after what happened this morning."

"Doctor Mackinaw is probably going to tell the police we were there, you know," I said.

"That's okay, I guess, so long as no one sees us. I'll feel better when we talk to Cal." Walter saw us walking toward him and gave us a honk. Jill started jogging slowly toward him.

"Well, girls, did you find out what you needed there?"

"More than we bargained for actually." I pinched Jill to remind her not to get Walter more involved than he already was.

"I tell you, Walt, when I finish this story I'm hoping it will at least get an honorable mention at *The Times-Picayune* awards night," Jill laughed.

"Nice to see you still have your dad's confidence." Walter chuckled. I knew Jill's dad from meeting him at her house a few times but had heard about him from his shrewd reputation around town. Thankfully I didn't have the experience to be in court against him. He represented more high-profile and serious cases outside the perimeter of the DA's office. He was a name brand in New Orleans, like many of the bigwigs around town. I'd heard of him before I'd met Jill and might have even seen him once at a law school event.

Maybe if Jill had gone along with her brothers into the family business, he wouldn't give her such a hard time—he hated that she was a reporter, or at least, that's what she told me.

"Jill, I gave Calvin a call and he's going to meet you at the house. I need to take care of a few more things in the garage so I need to get back anyhow. That okay with you?" Walt winked at us. I could tell that he was a good man, very loyal and kind.

"Walter, thanks for carting us around. We really appreciate it." I couldn't even imagine having someone like Walt working around my house. I'm sure Corrine knew what it was like now, but when we were growing up, we were responsible for chores like weeding, doing the dishes, making our beds and, then, doing our own laundry— after Mom had decided that we produced more laundry than she could handle! We used to share clothes and if we tried something on we'd put it in the laundry even if we hadn't worn it. It drove Mom crazy, but once we had to start doing the laundry ourselves we were more careful about that. I did Corrine's laundry as a swap for dishes, since she hated folding.

"You've gone over and above as usual. Heading back to the house is fine. Abby and I need to make a game plan." Jill wrote a few notes in the little notebook she always carried with her.

"Well, if there is anything else I can do to help, you let me know," said Walt as he turned the car back around towards the French Quarter.

"Walt, have you heard about any weird goings on over at Louis Armstrong Park?" I said, as Jill looked up from her scribbling.

"Well, it's not a park I'd really like to be hanging out in, but I've heard the cops had really straightened things out over there, in part due to the mayor's city beautification project."

"Do you know what they've done to clean it up?" I asked.

"Well, it's no secret that it's been a hooker and drug hangout, so

I think it's getting patrolled more often to clean it up. That's what I heard, anyhow, don't know for sure."

"Maybe you could drop us off there, and we could check it out. It's daytime. Nothing should happen in the daytime," Jill said.

"Oh, something can always happen in that park. You know better than that," Walt said.

"He's right, Jill, do you really think that's a good idea? We don't want to end up like one of those girls."

"What are you girls getting mixed up in?" Walt asked.

"No need to worry, Walt. I need to go there if I want to get the whole story. We don't have to stay long. After, we should stop at Covenant House and talk to them," Jill said.

"I think you should wait and go with Calvin, especially if you don't want to call the NOPD," Walter chimed in.

"Sounds like a plan," I said.

"We'll wait for Cal to go into the park, so if could you please drop us off just before Covenant House on Rampart." Walter abruptly turned to go down a different street to get us there. "We don't want to go to Covenant House with all those runaways there. They'll freak out if they see cops." I agreed. I had a lot of respect for them and had always wanted to be involved since I'd heard about it years ago.

"Even if we don't find out anything, going there will at least knock it off the list of where Darcy might be, then we can check out Deanna's later and follow the trail," Jill said.

"You know, Kermit is playing over at Deanna's tonight," Walt said.

"How do you know that?" I asked.

"Everybody knows that. It's Thursday. Look, it's right over there," he pointed.

"Okay if we jump out here? I think it's better if we walk the rest of the way down," Jill said. Walter pulled the Caddie over, and we hopped out. We thanked him, he waved, and drove away.

"You sure this is a good idea, Jill?"

"Abby, we can't stop now," Jill said.

"You're right, but let's be careful not to say too much. I wouldn't want to jeopardize Darcy's safety or ours."

"It'll be fine, Abby." Jill was right. A lot of theories were going through my head, but I couldn't help but be worried for our safety and Darcy's.

"Have you ever been to the Covenant House?" I asked Jill.

"Absolutely thought about running away from home but never did it."

"I wish I had a picture of Darcy so someone would know if they'd met her. Maybe she went along with your crazy plan and is sweating it out in Thailand as opposed to hiding out here in New Orleans."

"She'd better be or I'm a big sucker." Jill stepped over some cracked pavement nearby the house. We passed a few girls talking in the small courtyard area outside the main door.

"Excuse me, but we are looking for a friend who might have been staying here and carried a bag like hers." Jill pointed to my bag.

"Everyone's looking for someone." One of the girls seemed like she was trying to look tough because the others started giggling.

"Listen, we don't want to get anyone in trouble, but we're really worried about her. Have you heard of anyone here by the name of Darcy?" I hoped the mention of her name jogged their memory.

"*Darcy?*" The largest one of them took a step closer to us and stood with her arms akimbo. We both stepped back. "Why you want to talk to *Darcy?*"

Jill stepped forward again with her hand outstretched, and I put my hand on her shoulder to hold her back. I wasn't sure what she was going to do.

"I'm a friend. I'm Abby. She might have mentioned me if you talked to her. I only want to help her. Please tell us what you know about Darcy." I teared up without meaning to and wiped my eyes, but I wasn't willing to let a few girls bully us away. I told them the short version of the trial, what had happened, and why I was looking for Darcy.

"Abby, huh? You the lawyer lady? Yeah, she did say a few things about you."

CHAPTER 15

"I promise we won't get anyone in trouble. We just want to find Darcy and make sure she's safe," I said when a few of the girls started to walk away.

"Darcy felt real bad about what happened with the case and all. She knew it was important to you, and she wanted to help, but that judge and the cops…Man, that stinks for you, huh?" The bigger girl seemed to be the leader and corralled the girls into staying.

Another girl in a light blue hoodie said, "Darcy told me about you and all that stuff that happened in court with the judge and all. But she was happy, too, because she was—you know—scared and shit. That guy, well, he seems like a real bad guy, you know?"

"Anything else she told you?" I pressed.

"Hey, what's she writing? I don't want to get in trouble…." She pointed at Jill and started to walk away.

"I'm a reporter, and I'm not going to use any of your names. I just want to make sure I get my facts straight. You all will be famous, but nobody will know who you are. How about that?" Jill said.

"That sounds cool, I guess. Just don't go using any names. There's a code here, and we don't need you breaking it." The big girl puffed her chest out at Jill when she said this.

"Anything else you remember?" I asked the girl in the hoodie.

"I know she felt bad about lying to you. She said she needed to protect you...."

"Lied? What'd she lie about? Why'd she feel like she needed to protect me?"

"Um, well, she didn't really say. But it must have been something big because she wouldn't tell us. Then, she took off this morning without meeting us for breakfast downstairs."

"Any idea where is she now?" I was pacing. Everything they said made me question my every move.

"I'm not sure if she left for good, but if she comes back for dinner I can give her a note from you if you want," said the smallest girl there. She looked so young, but she was rocking a sleeping baby in a stroller.

"If you see her, please tell her to meet us at Deanna's at eight o'clock." Jill looked at her watch when she said this. "We have to go, but thank you, guys, for all your help." We needed to head back to the house to meet Calvin.

"Please make sure you tell her she's not in trouble. I only want to talk to her and make sure she's okay. Tell her it's Abby."

"I promise I won't forget." The girl picked up her crying baby and was rocking him in her arms, reminding me how lucky I was growing up.

"Make sure you tell her no one knows she's here except for us."

"How'd you even know where to look for her?"

"We found her bag at the morgue. Please tell her she needs to come meet us," Jill said.

"I'm counting on you guys. Please do what you can to get her the message," I said, as I handed them a few bucks. Jill tugged on my arm. We turned and started walking away from Rampart back into the Quarter towards Jill's house. I wasn't confident Darcy would show up at Deanna's. "Are you sure that was such a good idea to have her meet us at Deanna's?"

"She'll show," Jill said and walked a few steps ahead of me and answered her phone.

"I hope so," I said and checked my shirt for sweat marks. There was finally a slight breeze in the air. I could smell fried shrimp cooking and all I could think about was eating a po-boy.

Jill shoved her phone in her pocket and turned to me. "Deanna's is on her turf and close enough to where she's staying without invading her privacy. No one is going to see us there, and she'll know that."

"This is another bad plan, but I don't know what else to do. Do you think Calvin is going to be able to help us at all?" The pace of our walk was starting to make me sweat through my shirt again.

"Well, we can trust him. At this point, that's got to count for something." Jill said.

"If this doesn't pan out I'm going to go to my boss to see what else we can do," I said.

"That must be Calvin waiting out front." In front of her gate was a red car with a good-looking guy about our age leaning up against it. He wasn't wearing his uniform, but a white T-shirt and faded jeans. "Yo, Cal, hey you…" Jill ran up to him and gave him a big hug. He looked over at me, then to Jill. Then, he hugged her back in a way that made me know there had been something between them.

"When Uncle Walt called up and said you needed some of my expertise, I knew I had to make time for you." His voice curled around her like an embrace, and I swear I saw Jill swoon.

"This is Abby. I told you about her, right?"

I shook his hand. He laughed and gave me a little hug. "Any friend of Jill's is a friend of mine. Why don't we go inside and you guys can tell me what's up." He moved towards the gate.

"A cop—you know, I'm never going to get used to that," Jill flirted. I'd never seen her like this and was amused.

"You know, I could have been a lot of things, but I love being a cop, and I'm damn good at it, if I say so myself."

"Okay, Mister Cocky, Walt's already been bragging on you." Jill gestured over to the guest quarters. "Let's go over here so we stay out of everyone's way." Cal and I nodded and followed Jill to the little patio on the side of the main house with a small wrought-iron table and matching chairs. There was a vine-covered veranda over the table, which made it private. We all sat down.

Jill and I took turns telling Cal what had transpired at court and what we'd done. "I started looking into things a few weeks ago," she said and I glared at her. "You know, as a favor, and then when Abby had to go to New York for family stuff. I didn't intend to get so into it but I couldn't help myself." It was easy to talk to Cal, who seemed to hang on to our every word and scrunched his eyes when we told him a few of the crazy coincidences.

"Do you actually think this girl is going to show up tonight and give you all the answers?" Cal scratched his head. "Sounds like you're in a little bit over your head here. Abby, I'm really sorry about your dad, by the way."

"Cal, you're the only cop we've told because we're afraid that a few unsavory individuals within the department are involved. Shit, I got attacked at Abby's, so she can't even go back to her place! I'm sure by now my place is off limits, and what if they try to come here?"

"Listen, I have a friend over here in the NOPD who I know I can trust. Let me give him a call and see if there is any record of this case and the detectives working on it. Sounds like I should also get some info on the Maiden Voyage Club too."

"I know if Darcy's around she'll show up tonight. There is no way I completely misjudged her," I said, wanting to believe that was true.

Cal looked as if he didn't quite believe me. "I'm not on until ten, so I can go with you guys to make sure you're safe. If the girl shows up, then maybe I can help her."

"Can you call your friend at the NOPD now?" I asked.

"No problem," he said.

"Abby, come help me," Jill said as she got up and I followed her into the kitchen. She opened the fridge and took out a few beers.

"So, what's the deal with you and Calvin?"

"Yeah, okay, we used to have a thing when we were in high school and you know, once in a while since then. I mean, he can be such a player and Walt doesn't know at all, so you had better not say anything."

"When's the last time you saw him? You guys looked pretty friendly."

"I'm not sure—a while ago," she said and smiled coyly.

"How come Walt acted like you didn't connect?"

"He was joking. I had a big crush on him when I was younger. Of course, Walt teased me about it relentlessly. Cal and I used to play together all the time. Cal had a bad family situation, so he spent some years here with Walt and Vee."

"Is that why he wanted to be a cop?"

"Something like that. It wasn't like he had an abusive home life—just absentee parents. Walt thought Cal had a lot of potential, thought of him like a son. My dad treated him like another son too." Jill went into the kitchen and grabbed some chips and salsa.

"He seems nice," I said and thought about some of my own choices. Johnny wasn't a bad guy, but things had gotten so tangled up due to my stupidity with Jason and then the accident. I hadn't had a serious relationship since, but was thinking that I might be ready soon.

"Come on, let's go back over there and see if he found out anything." Jill handed me the Abita beers and a large jug of water while she carried everything else. Above anything else right now, I felt like I could use a beer. When we got back to the table, Cal was scribbling furiously in his notebook and saying uh-huh a lot. I set the beers down and pushed one toward him. He pushed it away and pointed to the water.

We couldn't help overhearing the conversation, especially when he said, "Special detail on *that* club? That's a little strange, isn't it?"

Jill and I looked at each other. I whispered, "Shoot, Jill—what are we going to do?"

"Great, you bet. Let me know when you find out anything else. I appreciate it. You have my cell." Cal hung up and poured himself a glass of water and gulped until he'd finished the whole thing.

"What's going on, Cal? What did you find out?" Jill sat down at the table. I grabbed the beer that Cal declined and chugged about half of it down when I didn't think they were looking.

"Either you guys have been lying to me, or someone is covering their tracks. There is no case by the state with a Chip Hebert or Darcy. And that Maiden Voyage Club is on some crazy special detail. It's kind of untouchable."

"There is no way this case is gone—impossible! Let me call my boss. I'm pretty sure I can trust him and he can find out." I took another sip of my beer.

"Hang on there, cowboy, I believe you. It's just that this doesn't add up from what you both told me." Cal grabbed a few chips and pushed them over to Jill.

"If I had known there was some serious shit going down when those cops came to your door, Abby, I never would have opened it. What if you were home?" Jill started to get into her manic-mode again, and I could tell she was furiously scribbling an article in her head.

"Cal, what do you think we should do to find out what is really going on?" I had a few ideas myself, but I was curious how a cop would handle it.

"Your friend, Darcy, seems like the only person that really might have an answer. If she trusts you, which it sounds like she does, my hope is that we get some answers when we see her at Deanna's."

"I want to go down there now and wait for her." I couldn't stand not knowing if Darcy was okay.

"Let me go upstairs to see if I can get online to see if there's a message from Val. I should have done that already," Jill said.

"I'm waiting on one more call, and then why don't we head over there now in case she comes early. It's almost seven now anyway." Cal started dialing again.

"I'll call the airline and give that one more shot." I headed inside the guesthouse for some privacy. I called the airline and the operator told me that they didn't give out that type of information even when I pleaded with them. I tried calling back to see if I could get an agent who would sympathize—same story; it was useless. I went back downstairs.

"I got nothing." I sat back down next to Cal and grabbed another beer. "You find out anything else?"

"Nothing, but I think we're on the right track." Cal grabbed the beer Jill was drinking and took a short swig. He reminded me of Jason, in the good ways.

Jill ran back over to us. "Val said she got to the airport and waited, but Darcy never arrived. She's definitely in New Orleans. I'm so stupid! She took the money and did something else with it!"

"I hope that doesn't make her a no-show." Cal looked frustrated with us.

"She's not like that, she'll show. Maybe she'll even have your money, Jill."

"Seems like you didn't really know this girl at all, Abby," Jill said.

"I can't believe that everything she told me was a lie. She'll show tonight, I know she will."

"It's early, but let's head on over anyway." Cal stood up from the table.

"I hope you're right, Abby, because this day cannot get any worse," Jill added.

"Another dead girl would be worse," I said and finished the last of my beer. I said a little prayer to my dad to help me and help Darcy to be brave and show up tonight.

"Hop in my car. I'll drive us over. Then I'll be able to go directly to work." We didn't argue and hopped in his red Jeep Cherokee, which was spotless. The ride probably took as long as walking due to the one-way streets. At a quarter of eight, we arrived at Deanna's to find ourselves the only customers in the bar, except for a few old guys who looked like fixtures rather than customers. The place was warm, and I could smell the savory smoky sausage simmering in the red beans and rice, which made my stomach grumble.

We sat down at a booth in the far corner from the door so we had privacy but could see people coming in. Cal went up to the bar and ordered. He didn't look like a cop—he was suave. Jill was squirming a bit in her seat, and I had started to tap my fingers on the table. It felt like we were counting down.

"Darcy is always late, so let's not get too stressed if she doesn't show up exactly at eight," I said as Cal arrived back at the table with Abita Ambers and placed them in the middle of the wooden table atop the red paper placemats. I pushed the salt, pepper, and hot sauces against the wall.

"I really hope she shows up," Cal said. Jill and I nodded. None of us had anything to say. We were all fixated on Cal's watch and the jumbo-sized clock over the bar. I forced myself to drink my beer slowly. Every time the front door opened—which wasn't much at this hour—the three of us jumped.

"She's not going to show," Jill said and I gave her the evil eye.

"If she's here, she'll show." I wanted this to be true so badly. If I had somehow jeopardized her life or gotten her killed, I wasn't sure I could forgive myself.

"I'm going to make a quick call to see if my buddy found out any more about the Maiden Voyage Club." Cal stood up. The door opened and we saw that it was the girl that Jill and I had had the conversation with in the front of Covenant House. She came right over to us.

"Where's Darcy?" I was stunned that she was here.

"That's what I came to talk to y'all about." She sat down at our table.

"What happened?" Jill lunged toward the girl and nearly grabbed her.

"Please tell me that you saw her and she's okay." I was trying not to be so maudlin and keep my cool.

"I need one hundred bucks, and then I'll tell you," the girl said as she crossed her arms. Disgusted, I pushed my chair back. Then, out of the corner of my eye, I saw the front door slowly open.

CHAPTER 16

I jumped up at the prospect of Darcy coming through the door, but it was just another woman with long brown hair. I was pissed at myself for even having spoken to this girl in front of Covenant House. We couldn't be sure if she had seen Darcy at all, or if she had, if she had told her about the meet. It *was* a stupid plan, and we'd dragged Cal along for the ride.

"We are not giving you any money. Why did you waste our time?" I slammed my hand on the table, I was so pissed.

"Your loss...." The girl got up and walked out of Deanna's. I was hoping that she'd turn around and tell us she'd been kidding and that Darcy was showing up. But it was already an hour after we had planned to meet. I felt like a fool.

While I was still brewing from the encounter, Jill was calm. "Sorry, Cal, for wasting your time. I was sure she was going to show up. When I saw her at Abby's apartment, she disclosed a lot of crazy shit to me, but I needed her to verify the truth. Now, I think she took the money I gave her and probably spent it. I'll let you know what happens, but it was good to see you." Jill's tone was coy and I expected she'd be yapping about him really soon.

"I can't believe I raced back home from a personal shitstorm merely to enter into another one here! What are we going to do now?" I didn't have the answers, nor did I think those guys did, but I was frustrated and felt like we'd come to a dead end.

"Listen, I need to go and head over to work. Call me if you find out something else or if you need me. I'll circle back with you if my sources come up with any more information. Jill, let's make it a point to connect tomorrow. I'm on the road until about six. Then, I'll go home and sleep for a few hours. Call me if you find something out, okay?" Cal stood up and gave Jill a kiss on the cheek. He was so cute and sweet. If there wasn't something between them, there should be. I was sorry that we'd wasted his time but glad those two had been able to connect.

"We'll get to the bottom of this, Cal, and then Jill will call you. Thanks for coming over with us and for your help." I put my hand out to shake, but he reached out and gave me a kiss on the cheek. His sweetness made me think of Johnny and what it would have been like had things not gone so wrong. I wanted to be with a nice guy in a normal relationship with no drama.

"Well, what are we supposed to do now? I'm at a complete loss, but I probably need to tell you some of the crap I found out talking to Darcy and see if you can shed some light." Jill drew her chair to face mine.

"You're starting to freak me out again, Jill." Then I looked over Jill's shoulder and saw Darcy walking toward us from the kitchen. My jaw dropped: "Holy shit, I can't believe it." Behind her was the girl who'd tried to extort the hundred dollars from us.

Jill turned around. "So, she wasn't lying."

Darcy walked over and sat down. "Sorry, I sent Keesha over here to scout things out after she told me you guys were looking for me. I wanted to make sure that it was really you. She was going to give you the money back if you gave it to her. A lot of weird shit has been going on, and I didn't want to take any chances."

Darcy told us how she got to her apartment to find it tossed and got nervous, and the only place she could think of going was to see me. Heading out of the country seemed like a crazy idea to her, so she did what she thought was the next best thing and checked into Covenant House. She told them she was from St. Louis, which was true, and that she had run away and that someone was trying to hurt her. I'm sure they assumed she was involved with some kind of john, but they were good about not asking too many questions to spook the girls. Luckily, they had space for her for a few days.

"I didn't want to spend Jill's money on a hotel, and there's no way anyone would look for me here. How you guys even find me?" I thought about describing our trip to the morgue, but didn't want her to freak out until she told us the whole story.

The girl left as soon as Darcy sat down at our table and said she'd see her later. "I'm so glad that you told Abby we were working together. Now, we can really bring this place down, and I can quit hiding out." Jill looked at her when she said this and shook her head, then put her head down.

"Jill, what is she talking about? I thought the first time you guys met was when Darcy came to my apartment, and you gave her money to go to Thailand? Tell me what's really going on around here or I'm going to call the cops."

"Please, let me explain. I was going to tell you but I wanted all of us to be together and to make sure that Darcy was okay."

"Jill, you've got to quit playing fucking FBI on me and tell us what the hell is going on. First, you tell me that you've sent Darcy off to Thailand to see Val, and then, you…"

"She did tell me to go to Thailand and give me money, but I didn't want to go. If I could lay low around here, maybe I could help a bit more with the investigation."

"What the hell are you two talking about?" I felt as mad as I did when Darcy wasn't taking the case seriously, but it felt worse because I thought Jill was my best friend.

Jill told us that, at dinner one day, her father had been talking about scumbag clients in his office after hours. He mentioned one of his clients, a strip club owner, was a cheat, and he was angry at himself for getting involved with him. "Nothing gets me worse than when someone lies to me. You want to write a story, Jill, write a story about a scumbag like that," he'd told her. She was surprised that someone had gotten under his skin enough for him to erupt in front of her, even more so that he even suggested she write a story about it. From what I knew, he was a defense lawyer who worked on a lot of class-action lawsuits and a variety of local bread-and-butter cases, along with some maritime law, so being involved with a criminal case was a surprise to me.

Jill continued, "You know, occasionally, I do freelance work for my dad. It helps me keep current on my rent, so I don't feel like such a mooch."

"Nope, you didn't mention this to me, Jill. I think I might have remembered that."

"Well, it's no big deal, you know. It helps me pay my rent rather than just plain asking him for money and getting the third degree. And it also gets him off my back about working with my brother— or worse—going to law school!"

"And here I thought you just had a nice allowance. That's cool," I said.

"I started reading some of the documents I was photocopying as part of the discovery. I wanted to know what my dad was so pissed about. I found the Maiden Voyage stuff, and then it made sense." The guy her dad had spoken about owned or had his hand in a lot of businesses around town.

"But, Jill, it's not like you could use any of that information in your reporting, right? I mean, they'd know where you got it from."

"Yeah, and Dad would have killed me, so I needed to do my own investigation over the past few months. I wanted to figure out exactly who the client was and which club he owned without jeopardizing Dad by divulging his confidentiality. Then, of course, I'd have a paper trail."

"I still don't understand what this has to do with Darcy." I was trying to think back over the clues I must have missed that would have lead me to this information. I guess I was so concerned with felonies that I may have overlooked the obvious.

"Abby, I was feeling paranoid after the case and how it went down," Darcy said as she twirled her hair around her index finger. "It was just so crazy and even though Chip would be insane to try and get back at me, I didn't feel safe, so I went to your house, and Jill was there. We talked for a long time. I felt so bad about your dad. Jill got us a few beers and I told her everything I knew."

"Darcy, you should have called me."

"I wanted to talk in person, Abby. It would come out better that way."

"Well, I was really frustrated with how my little investigation was going," said Jill. "I combed through public documents, talked to a variety of people downtown, and hung out at a ton of bars down in the Quarter to see if I could find out anything. It was a pipe dream that a guy like that would leave any tracks, that is, until Darcy told me about the kind of stuff she was doing with the club's accounting, along with the office in Harahan."

"Abby, I didn't think it was important to tell you I worked there, especially since my paystubs said MVP Restaurant Group and you seemed to be okay with that and not ask any more questions. I didn't want to make an issue out of it. I didn't want you to think any less of me. I worked the bar a few nights and did some bookkeeping a few afternoons per week, so basically what I told you was mostly true. I'm friends with a few of the girls who dance, and they were always trying to talk me into it for the money."

"Darcy, I'm not sure I can believe you at this point." I was trying hard not to be angry, but I felt betrayed. I also felt like an idiot because I'd neglected to probe something so elementary and critical to my case, which made me feel like a complete failure.

"That's all true, Abby," said Jill.

"I don't know if I can believe you either, Jill," I said. I thought about Nola and how sad Darcy was going to be when she found out. I could tell that Nola was a good girl, and I didn't know what she had done to end up at the morgue. I knew if we weren't careful it was likely that one of us would be next.

"Darcy, after all that time we spent together, it hurts that you felt like you couldn't trust me. I wouldn't judge. You know that." I felt hurt that she had felt comfortable enough to confide in Jill, but not me.

"I actually thought it might be better if you didn't know because you'd have to tell someone and the police would definitely be involved in a way that would make it messy." Darcy reached into a small black purse and pulled out a lip gloss.

"Well, I'm not so sure about that, nor am I really sure we shouldn't involve the police now," I said, although at this point, Cal was the one person I thought I could trust.

"Listen, I didn't plan on uncovering what I did. I mean, like, how would I plan on someone trying to threaten me, but here we are," Darcy said, grabbing my beer and guzzling the rest of it.

Darcy started detailing her jobs at the club: answering phones in the office, filing paperwork, and organizing the billing for the accountant. After she'd been working there for about a year, the boss told her he had some other little jobs for her. He said he'd pay time-and-a-half for this work if she'd keep it completely confidential. He called it "high priority." She started the extra work helping the accountant. She showed Darcy how the books needed to be kept for each of his businesses. There was small-business-loan money, and they needed to adjust and finish the paperwork. She gave Darcy a stack of files and told her how to do the first application. Then she asked her to do the same for the other applications so they could be submitted to an office out in Harahan.

"At the time, I needed the money. Besides, they were nice to me, and it didn't feel weird at all. It was better than dancing, which I completely sucked at, okay? I haven't tried it again since, if you care to know."

"What is actually *in* Harahan? I've never even heard of the place." I wanted to keep on point so I didn't get irritated again at her about the dancing or not-dancing lies.

"I had to go to an industrial park where they had some storage for some of the stores and properties. They were paying me $15 an hour plus time-and-a-half, including my drive time, so it was a sweet situation because I also had my shifts at the bar. Now I could pay for school and still have time to study and do the sorority gig. Honestly, I didn't care where they sent me as long as I was getting paid, but it became kinda obvious something wasn't right. The girl who worked there and I got friendly. She said it was a genius operation because not only did they set up small businesses to get business loans, but once they got them, some older ones would have to go bankrupt. There was always money coming in and out." I thought, that must have been why the scams had little chance of being detected. The operation was run like a business.

"Jill, how did you plan on putting a stop to this without getting the police involved?" I pushed my chair back from the table.

"Abby, I only wanted the story. Then I was going to give it to the police. I had narrowed things down to a few clubs. After I spoke with Darcy, I knew the Maiden Voyage must be the club my dad mentioned. It was a weird coincidence, but it made sense. Problem was that I determined that we couldn't really go to the police since many of the officers were actually involved."

"When I figured out that they were setting up dummy

corporations and actual office space in the industrial park in Harahan, I knew I couldn't work there anymore," Darcy said. "I wasn't interested or comfortable being involved with anything illegal. I tried to quit—but I knew too much. Then it got even worse...."

"What about our case? I don't understand how all of that would play into any of this." Darcy explained how it was merely a fluke that Chip's dad had any connection to the case at all. What she told me had been true, that she had liked Chip, thought he liked her and then Chip had turned out to be a psycho because he knew she was working at the club and considering leaving. What she didn't know at the time was that Chip's dad was a partner in the club. "The girl in the Harahan office ratted me out to Chip that I was going to leave. So, on that night he started off trying to convince me to stay, and you know how that ended."

"Darcy, why didn't you tell me all this? Maybe we could have notified the police and they could have put a stop to this."

"When Chip came at me and told me I'd better not fuck around with my job, I threatened to go to the police. That's when Chip went ballistic. We'd had sex once before, but this time he tried to force himself on me. I told him to stop and he wouldn't. It was horrible. He hit me so hard I passed out. I jolted awake when he was dragging me, but I was afraid if I started to fight he might hurt or even kill me. So, when he stopped I laid down with my hands over my head. Then, he kicked me hard in the head. I got woozy and had to shut my eyes so I wouldn't throw up.

"Then, I woke up in the park and that's about when you found me. I felt so shitty and humiliated, but you were so nice to me. I thought I could get back at Chip and get out of the whole situation, but when that judge went away like that I knew that this was more than I could control. I was scared and I don't think you would have believed me anyhow."

She told us how she started to feel paranoid like everyone was following her, which is why she spent a lot of time in my office. She trusted me, but was afraid to tell me much because it might only get her in more trouble. Then, after the judge got taken away, she kept seeing this one guy following her. She'd see him at work, and then, after she gotten home, she'd see the same car idling down the block. The girls she helped weren't staying at her apartment any more. She wondered if they'd been picked up and told on her. "I went to your apartment to tell you everything. When you weren't there, I just spilled everything to Jill. I couldn't keep it a secret any longer."

Jill chimed in: "I was afraid the police were involved, especially with what had happened to the judge, so I was trying to figure out what to do. I thought about talking to my dad, but knew he'd get pissed off when he found out who I was investigating. Then, Val called looking for you. After I told her about your dad and everything, she suggested that Darcy go away until this was all sorted out."

Jill should have been a lawyer, I thought. She had an insightful way of looking at things. Darcy was picking at her chipped red nail polish, which was almost completely gone.

"Why didn't you tell me Jill? Why go on this wild goose chase today to find Darcy?"

"I honestly figured the less you knew the safer you would be until we knew that Darcy was okay."

"Well, I wish you hadn't really gotten me involved now because I have a duty to take this information to the DA to go after these guys now." I rubbed my fingers on my temple. I was worried about proof, though, and the fact that since powerful people were involved it might be difficult to find anything that linked them to the scam. It bothered me that Jill was on this quest behind my back; I thought we were better friends than that. And, I felt very hurt by Darcy's lies, but not surprised.

"There's a little bit more—Harahan is actually where a lot of provision companies are. You know, the ones that deliver goods to the ships on the Mississippi." Darcy told us how one day the Polish shipping company next door asked if she could give a ride to a few girls who were going back to the club. "The girls seemed about my age and only spoke Polish until they got in the car. Once they got in, they used their broken English to tell me how they had come on one of the ships and that a woman had told them they could have a job. One of them was crying, saying she'd been raped aboard. The guy told her that once she started working there was going to be more where that came from so she'd better get used to it."

According to the girls, that kind of thing happened repeatedly during the entire journey. They begged Darcy not to take them back to the club. This all happened the week before the case went to trial.

"Where are the girls? Why did you keep working there when you saw what was happening?" I said. "Did you give one of the girls your big messenger bag you always carry?" I looked at Jill when I said this, but she was writing something down.

"I gave it to one of the girls that was staying with me as a swap for this one. I had spilled a little polish on it, so it was time for a new one."

I looked at her funny. "Which girl is staying with you?" I wanted to at least help Doctor Mackinaw identify the missing girl with Darcy's bag. Jill looked at me when I said this. Her cheeks were flushed, either by the emotion of the situation or simply the beer.

"I didn't really have a choice. By working there, I was showing my loyalty even though the case was continuing. I told them you were never going to let it go, but that I would do my best to cooperate without giving up any additional information about the club. I don't think they believed me when I said the girls ran away. At that point, I wasn't going to go back there anymore. After the girls stayed at my apartment for a few days, I gave them some clothes, some other stuff, and part of the money you gave me to get them started. I didn't know what else to do. I told them I could go to the police, but they were afraid of getting deported."

"Did they think you were a complete idiot? I can't believe they would have let you near those girls to drive them in the first place," I said.

"Knowing that the case was continuing and that I had confirmed I wasn't interested in making any waves, they figured I wouldn't ask any questions. After all, the girl at the office over there assured me that it was fine, like a student exchange program. They weren't kidnapped or anything. The girls were promised jobs with room and board, but didn't know that they were going to be dancers, so maybe it wasn't that bad. But the more I thought about it, the more unsavory I realized it was. I took it upon myself to tell them what was going on and the looks on their faces told me that was not what they had envisioned when they were told there would be work."

As Darcy spoke, Jill was busy writing notes. If I hadn't been so overzealous, then maybe I could have avoided this big mess. Jill, on the other hand, was engrossed. This was the big story she'd been looking for!

"Abby, I want to figure this out as much as you and Darcy do. I want to bust these people with whatever they are illegally doing with the money, and, of course, the girls. Where are they now, Darcy? Do you know?" Jill had put down her pen at this moment and was looking at Darcy intently as she spoke.

"You were so good to me, Abby, and I liked talking with you. I didn't feel like it was fair to get you involved in this mess." Darcy wiped away a tear.

"Darcy, what happened to the girls? Do you know where they are?" When Jill said this, Darcy put her hands on her face and started to cry. I scanned the room—no one seemed to be paying us any attention.

"I think I did something really bad, really bad…." Darcy choked through the words

CHAPTER 17

I t took about fifteen minutes for us to calm Darcy down and to get her to even think about telling us what happened to the girls. "If you didn't harm them, then you didn't do anything wrong," I assured her. I couldn't imagine that she had hurt anyone, let alone the girls she was trying to help.

"I shouldn't have gotten involved; I should've taken them where I was supposed to." She was having trouble breathing between sobs. "But they were so scared!"

"Darcy, let me tell you the facts here. Someone is trying to hurt us, all of us, it seems. You are making it more difficult for us to figure things out so we can stop this from happening. I know Abby is not going to get you in trouble for saying what you need to say. Right, Abby?"

"Unless you personally caused them some serious physical harm, which I don't think you did, then nothing can be held against you, I promise." I hoped to God she didn't tell me something that was going to make me wish I had eaten those words. In my gut, I knew that she'd only tried to help the girls.

She wiped her tears and said, "I brought the girls back to my house. Then, I didn't know what to do. They didn't have any money, they didn't want to go home, and they didn't want to go with this guy Frank and work at the Maiden Voyage. That's why I was late that morning, but I couldn't tell you why."

"If you had told me, I could have helped you." I wanted to shake her, but I knew she did the best she could. The waitress came over, I asked for another round of beers, and then nodded for Darcy to continue.

"I rushed back after court to make sure they weren't having any trouble and Nola was there talking to them. She was trying to convince them that it wasn't so bad. It was an opportunity for work, and, besides, there was going to be some serious shit going on if they didn't go back. When I got there, Nola pulled me aside and told me that if they didn't go back we were both going to be in big trouble. Nola was pissed at me because now she felt like she was in on it too. She didn't tell me any of this when I got the job. I just thought it would be a way to make a lot of money. Besides, I was just an errand girl. But I'm not stupid, I knew that it wouldn't last."

"Did you send the girls back there with Nola?"

"I had to. She said they would kill her if she didn't bring them back. We argued a little, but then two of them agreed to go back with Nola. But, Bronia...well, she wasn't as pretty as the other girls, so she decided she would take her chances."

"You risked your own safety by helping these girls. You could have been the one that ended up murdered in the park." I didn't want to lecture her, but without malice and unknowingly, she'd contributed to the situation. I felt awful about Nola, but I needed to tell her.

"I've been kind of freaking out since then because Nola was supposed to come back to my place and let me know the girls were okay. Instead, she left this freaky message that I needed to get out of my place, that it wasn't safe. Bronia and I went over to Covenant House, hoping that they would have a bed for each of us, and they wouldn't ask too many questions, which they didn't. I'd never been in a place like that. It was sad. There were some very young girls that had obviously run away and been living on the streets. I felt a little guilty for going there, but I didn't have the money to do anything else. In fact, here is the rest of your money," Darcy said and handed Jill a wad of bills that she had had folded in her pocket.

Jill didn't look to count it. She just said thanks and put it in her bag. "So, what happened when you got there?"

"We just laid low. We didn't decide not to talk to anyone, but I either left my phone at my house or someone swiped it, so I was without contact for a few days, which probably made Nola insane. I didn't want to go back to my place until I figured out what to do." She told us how she felt like she couldn't even trust Nola at this point and wanted nothing to do with girls being put in a club like that against their will. "I don't care how much they wanted to pay me to do that. I can't believe I'd been so stupid. I was so clueless and if I'd looked I'm sure I could have noticed that something was wrong. Certain rooms and offices were absolutely no entry and they were guarded by guys with guns." She said when she asked Nola, she warned her to just focus on the money.

I was so engrossed in the story I didn't notice more people trickling into the bar for red beans and rice, which, we were told, the owner's husband had cooked up. The room was filled with the aromas of Andouille sausage and spices, and I was tempted to get a plate myself. "You know, Darcy, Nola called me in New York because she was worried about you," I said.

"She probably thought I talked to you about it even though I swore I didn't. I don't remember giving her your number. What did she say when you spoke with her? Before I left my apartment, I did leave a message with her to let her know where I was staying."

"Do you think she told anyone else where you might be staying?" Jill looked at me: We knew we had to tell Darcy what happened.

Darcy shook her head. "How the heck did you find me? That's

what's sort of freaking me out. If nobody else knew, how did you find me?" She pushed her chair back and stood up. Then, she bent down to find her shoes under the table and bumped her head on the way up. "Shit!" The waitress came back to drop off the beers; I handed her a twenty and told her to keep it.

"Darcy, sit for a few more minutes. We have to tell you something," I said, grabbing her arm as she tried to walk away. "I got called back from New York because I needed to go to the morgue and identify a body. Nola had called me telling me she couldn't find you." My voice shook a little when I spoke.

Darcy cried, "Is it Nola? Is Nola the one at the morgue?"

"I'm so sorry, Darcy," I said and put my hand on her wrist. She crumpled to the floor and started to hyperventilate.

"Darcy, come on, please, we can't make a scene," Jill said and got her up into a chair.

Darcy steadied her breathing and said, "Just tell me what happened. I need to know."

"They found Nola's body in Louis Armstrong Park. When we went to the morgue, Jill recognized her. I'm so sorry. There was another girl too, maybe one of the Polish girls? She had a messenger bag like yours." Darcy gasped and her lower lip began to quiver. "I'm pretty sure it was your bag anyhow; it had a nail polish stain just like you said." I put my arm around her and she shook but didn't cry. Then, she shook harder and grabbed onto me. I told her it was going to be okay, even though I knew that it wasn't. I still felt bad for her, despite everything that she'd done.

"Where is Bronia?" I nearly whispered when I said this, but we had to know.

"I gave her some of your money and now she's on a bus to visit some cousins in Michigan. After we got to Covenant House we talked about what to do. Her English wasn't that bad; she'd obviously studied it. She told me that she didn't know the girls other than their names: Kasia and Lettie. They were from some city in Poland that I hadn't heard of and had been told that they would get good jobs. It was too late once they were on that big grain ship, which was like a locker room of horny sailors. Bronia didn't care about the other two girls, she wanted to go find her cousins, which had always been her plan when she'd saved up enough money to pay her contract out for getting here. She seemed more pissed off that she wouldn't be making any of the money she was promised. She called her cousins and they told her to take the bus, but they didn't have any money to send her so I helped her."

Darcy told us she contacted her mother to see if she could go for a visit to St. Louis, but her mother said that her new boyfriend wanted to go on vacation so she wasn't going to be home. It made me think about my mom and if she would ever have a boyfriend or relationship after Dad. Darcy talked about how stupid she was to think Nola was her only true friend and how she felt like she didn't fit in with regular girls, especially at her sorority. I felt sorry for Nola, she'd gotten herself in a difficult predicament and paid the ultimate price.

"We have to go get that other girl!" Darcy gasped between tears. "They are going to kill her too! And then they are going to find me. What am I going to do? Where am I supposed to go?" Darcy took a sip of the beer in front of her and scrunched up her face, pushing it away.

"My friend Cal is with the Jefferson Parish police, you just missed him. He'll help us," Jill said.

"It's true, Darcy, we can trust him." I didn't think it would do any good to mention that she would have met Cal if she hadn't shown up so late.

"The cops are in on it, we can't tell him— they'll know where I am!" Darcy calmed herself down to a whisper. The band was starting to jam and more people were starting to filter into Deanna's.

"What do you mean the cops are in on it?"

"The cops that took away the judge from our case are some of the same ones that hang around the Maiden Voyage Club. How do you think that place fell off the radar? Everyone is receiving a cash payoff. The club is the cash cow to pay for it all. So long as there is a constant flow of different pretty girls no one can get suspicious—that is the genius of it. The cops help facilitate this and the various partners are part of different partnership conglomerates that make up the businesses running out of the Harahan offices."

"How did you figure it out?" I asked, trying to hide my incredulity.

"Honestly, they keep you so petrified that they might hurt you, you don't want to say anything to anybody. Why do you think I didn't tell you any of this shit before, Abby? I didn't want to get you involved. I mean, the whole situation with Chip was a message. Even though it seemed like it had nothing to do with the club, I don't believe that now. They wanted me to keep quiet, but you wouldn't let me do that. I'm grateful for that, but I didn't want you to know more than you needed to because I was afraid for *my* life. And, if I told you, I'd be afraid for *your* life as well, and I couldn't deal with that."

Darcy went on to tell us how she'd become suspicious a few months ago and started making a few extra copies of paperwork. After Jill tried to convince her to leave the country, Darcy even hid a little backup information in a safety deposit box at the Hibernia bank right near my apartment on that day she went to see me.

"Darcy, if you had told me, I could have done something. The last thing I'd want to do is put you in danger." I did feel guilty for putting Darcy in jeopardy, since I also had selfish motives that I'd get some clout around the office if I won the case.

"Listen, why don't the three of us go back to my parents' place and get some rest? Cal is working, so we can't do anything right now but I'll leave him a message. We'll take this information to the goddamned FBI if we have to."

"I need to go check out at Covenant House. I agreed to stay for the night. If they don't hear from me, the gals I met there might get worried." Darcy used a bar napkin to wipe the mascara that had run under her eyes.

"You gave your real name to those girls at Covenant House, didn't you?" I thought about Keesha and our encounter earlier in the day.

Darcy looked at me when I said this and her face went white. "I can't go back there now, can I?"

"No. No, you can't," Jill said as she stood up. The band was doing a sound check and eating red beans and rice before the set.

"Too bad we can't stay...." Darcy looked over at the band. "Remember I told you the best night to be here? Well, it's Kermit Ruffin's night, and we're going to miss it. How ironic is that?" She tried to laugh, and I forced a little smile. Nothing I liked better than a buzz and some good music, but tonight wasn't the night. Kermit was warming up on his horn and I could hear why people loved him. But, the seriousness of our situation was palatable and what little we could do would have to wait until the morning. On the way out, Darcy caught Kermit's eye and waved. He waved back. He hadn't even started, but he already looked like he was having a good time!

We got back to Jill's and all headed upstairs. "I'm going to stay up a bit and write so both of you should take the other room," she said. "I'll set an alarm to wake us up at a reasonable hour. We'll go first thing and get those documents you stashed at the bank." Jill seemed insistent. The documents were all she could talk about since Darcy told us about them.

"I know I'm going to have a hard time sleeping." I had too much on my mind and my brain was racing. I set another alarm on my phone. Between thoughts of what was going on, I wondered if Johnny would ever call me back. If I learned anything from this mess, I learned the value of telling the truth.

The house got quiet and all I could hear was the rustling of sheets for a few minutes before silence. I turned off our light and fell asleep to the rhythmic sounds of Darcy's heavy breath.

After what felt like a minute later, I woke up with a start, almost unable to catch my breath. I looked at the clock on my phone and saw that it was quarter past two. Darcy was still breathing heavy, and the light was still on in Jill's room. I tried to shut my eyes, but I felt completely awake, realizing I'd fallen asleep with all my clothes on. I'd had the same dream that I'd had many times before over the past few months, except this time, I'd changed the ending. In these dreams, I ran as fast as I could through streets that reminded me of Venice (they were like a labyrinth), but I never discovered where I was going or who was chasing me. However, this time, I turned around, waiting to confront who was chasing me—I woke myself up and had to catch my breath.

I was careful getting out of bed; I didn't want to wake Darcy. I walked over to where Jill was sleeping in the other room to see if she was still working. Jill was sleeping with the light on and her laptop next to her on her bed. As I crept over to turn off the light, I was tempted to go on her computer and read what she'd written so far. I went back to my room and decided since I was awake that this wouldn't be the worst time to go and get my car, if it was still by the hospital and hopefully not towed. I grabbed my bag and my phone and started walking downstairs and stopped when the stairs creaked as loud as a crow's squawk. I listened but I didn't hear any movement from Jill or Darcy, so I carefully continued down the stairs. I stepped outside on the patio. The air felt comfortable, much cooler than in the heat of the day but still thick with humidity.

While walking to the gate, I thought it might be a good idea to call Cal again. He would be up since he was working and maybe he'd be able to give me a little insight into what we'd found or at least some advice on what we should do. I wanted to call in the brigade and bust down the Maiden Voyage Club and the illegal Harahan office, but understood that would not be easy with a corrupt police force protecting the accomplices. If I approached the situation like that I was bound to be the next missing person found in Louis Armstrong Park.

When I called Cal, he picked up right away and said, "Hey." He had a nice voice, clear and strong, almost like one of those narrative commercials on the radio, and it was exactly like he sounded in person.

"It's Abby, Cal, sorry to bug you, but I couldn't sleep and there is a lot of shit going on. Do you have time to talk for a minute? Did you get Jill's message?"

"I did. You guys really got yourselves in quite a mess, didn't you? I took a short shift so I could help you, but I couldn't do much except make a few calls since I was on duty. I'm getting off in a little bit, and I was planning to connect with some of my sources," he said above his police radio that was humming directions that made it difficult to hear him clearly.

"The girls are asleep, but I wanted to pick up my car and maybe head downtown for a bit."

"Don't be stupid, Abby. I'll swing over to you in less than thirty. I'd rather be on my own, but I can tell from your voice that you're going to go out no matter what I say, so we might as well go together. Then, at least you'll be safe."

"Did you find out anything else?"

"I'll tell you when I get there." He hung up. I sat down at the outside table and put my knees up into my shirt and rocked. I couldn't go back to sleep now; I had to find out what he knew.

CHAPTER 18

·•◦•═══════•═══════•◦•·

I heard Cal at the front gate before I saw him. I ran over and hoped that the dogs were inside so they wouldn't start barking. I didn't want to risk waking the whole house up.

"Cal, I'll come out to you," I said in a hushed tone. Since we were still in the Quarter, it was never completely quiet. We were in a less trafficked area, but somehow the Quarter still hummed even more than during the day. I knew from personal experience that some evenings just get started at 3 a.m., and strange things happened in the wee hours, especially in the Quarter. I got outside the gate and could see Cal was in his plain clothes again and with his own car. "How'd you get out so early?"

"I told my boss I had a lead on something outside of scope and asked if I could take a few hours of lost time to pursue it or drop it. My partner said he could manage the paperwork, and I'll double up for him next time. No big deal."

"Darcy had some documentation of the illegal activities going on at the Maiden Voyage Club held in a safety deposit box that we can access in the morning. What did you find out?" I pushed my hair behind my ear. I hoped I didn't look too ragged. Cal was so poised; I felt self-conscious.

"Darcy actually showed up? Damn, I wish I had been able to wait. What else did she tell you? Why didn't Jill call me?" He was a little snappish when he said this, but then bobbled his head and said, "I'm a little tired, don't mind me." I quickly recapped our conversation at Deanna's about one girl going to Michigan but the other, if she were still alive, should be at the Maiden Voyage Club. I told him about the illegal businesses, the money laundering, and the offices in Harahan.

Then Cal said that his source at the FBI had been investigating the club for months, but hadn't been able to make a break in the case. "Sounds like there were a lot of partners and a lot of cops involved, so they may have been waiting to make a big sting. Since those two girls had been found dead, they had also been looking for Darcy. With the information they gathered, the FBI knows that she is the one person involved who has no known criminal liability."

"How can they be so sure?"

"Nola was actually an informant, so she knew that Darcy was clean. She wasn't sure until Darcy didn't bring the girls over to the club as Nola had expected. Unfortunately, Darcy's heroic act of trying to help the girls compromised the integrity of the investigation. Nola was killed before she could bring all the information to her connection. She was found in the park near Covenant House, so we can assume she may have been going over to see Darcy, since she was the only person that could have known where she was."

"How do you know all this? I thought you were just a cop in Jefferson? I don't mean, just a cop, but you know what I mean." I hadn't meant to insult Cal, but he looked at me sternly. When I tried to backpedal, he chuckled.

"I do have a lot of connections around here. Now you can't expect me to reveal all my sources, can you?"

"What do we do now? They're going to kill that other girl, aren't they?"

"I sure hope not, but that is a possibility. I think they killed the other one as a warning and trust me, they don't want that whole 'shipment' to be a loss so I don't think they are going to kill her. As for Nola, unfortunately, I think she got killed because she was trying to protect Darcy. Nola must not have seen it coming or someone would have been there to back her up."

"Do they have enough evidence to shut the place down?"

"They are afraid to move in too quickly and upset all the hard work Nola and some of the other undercover officers put in. This investigation has been going on for about a year and involves a lot of people."

"I could go in there looking for Nola or Darcy. Wouldn't that make sense that I'd want to see her upon getting back into town?" I got into Cal's car. He put in the key and turned down the radio, which was on WOOZ, my favorite station.

"I think that's too risky, and it doesn't make sense. What I'd like to do right now is go over to your apartment and see if we missed anything. Where did you keep the case file?"

"I keep all that stuff in my office. I don't take anything home unless I'm working on it. I don't want to be responsible for losing anything."

"Then we need to head over to your office and grab that file. Do you have access after hours?"

"I do…you think that it's a good idea to go over there *now*? I don't know if I feel comfortable with that."

"I think considering that file might give us a little more insight as to how your office might be involved, a quick search on your database might offer us some connections, unless you can think of any off the top of your head?"

"The only thing I can think of was that my boss wasn't too keen on my moving forward with the case, but I thought it was because he wanted a quick plea out rather than a trial. I was the one who wanted to take this one all the way. I don't think anyone could have stopped me." I directed Cal where to turn to get to the parking lot for my office. We were close and I had the key since I had brought it with the intention of getting my car back. I'd gotten special permission for after hours' access. I'd been spending so much time on Darcy's case that I needed to put in additional time to keep up with my other cases. I still had reservations. "Shouldn't we tell the FBI about it? I mean, if they are looking at this situation, I don't want to step on anyone's toes."

"Abby, I know you haven't known me for very long, but do you trust me?" Cal looked over at me and then back to the road.

After he said this, I stared at him and thought about what I felt in my gut when I met him. It only took me a few seconds to respond: "Actually, I do." On the other hand, I *was* starting to get concerned that Jill and Darcy still knew more about this than they were telling me. But, for the moment, and from what very little I knew about Cal, there was something about *him* that felt sane. Maybe it was his demeanor. Maybe it was Walt's faith in him or how he seemed so steadfast in his loyalty to being a cop (but not actually like a regular cop). At this point, I had to trust someone and Cal seemed like my best shot of feeling safe while this got sorted out.

After we got near my office's parking lot, I changed my mind and told him to park around the corner from the building. That way, if the cameras were on in the parking lot, they wouldn't record our car. There was a back way into the office that a lot of the ADAs used as a smoking area, because there were no working cameras there. We parked and then hustled over to the building. We wanted to get in and out before the first security guards arrived at the door. The door opened easily, and I led the way to my office on the third floor. I was feeling buzzed from adrenaline or perhaps the few sips of coffee I'd had in Cal's car. Thankfully, he said he always got coffee after work to make sure he didn't fall asleep on his way home.

"Follow me." I hooked a right into the stairwell and started climbing the stairs. Even though we weren't doing anything wrong,

I thought it best not to engage the elevators. We walked into my office, and I stopped dead in my tracks.

"What happened? Hurricane hit this place?"

"I didn't leave it like this. Looks like someone has been rifling through my stuff!"

"Where do you keep your files?"

"I only keep active files in my desk; the rest I stored in a cabinet down the hall. Darcy's should still be here because I wasn't finished." I looked through the files on top of my desk, which were completely out of order. If I hadn't known better, I would have thought someone was trying to take over a few cases for me in my absence. However, this looked like someone had been looking for something but couldn't find it. While I was looking for the file, Cal was booting up my computer so we could get online.

"Password?"

I leaned over his shoulder to get a look at the computer. Cal must have taken a shower at work because he still smelled like clean laundry. Then, I gave him a little shove, shooing him away from the keyboard. "Girl's gotta have some secrets." I typed in my password. "Doesn't look like the file is here anymore."

I moved back over to see if the paper file might be on the floor, while Cal tried to infiltrate the system to find whatever connection he was looking for. I walked down the hall to the big file cabinet to see if the file had been put away.

I scouted around my section and couldn't find it. Then, I went over to Bruce's desk. "Shit!" I said aloud, as I jiggled the door. I went over to Bruce's secretary's desk to see if I could find the key I'd seen her put in there. I found it, ran over, and started scanning through the drawer when Cal yelled, "Abby, come over here quickly!" I ran back over to the office and stared at the computer screen with him. "Look, it's all right here!" I looked at the screen and the list of cases that he'd generated. At first, I didn't understand the connection, but then it dawned on me.

"Oh, my God!" was all that I could say when I realized exactly what connected these files.

CHAPTER 19

"**D**o you think Jill knows?" When I connected the dots as to what Cal had just showed me, I couldn't believe it. "Why do you think her dad wanted her to think that he wouldn't be involved with people like that and this sort of thing? The way it's looking, he must have deliberately led her on a wild goose chase, but that seems too crazy!" The list Cal had produced showed that the Maiden Voyage Club had generated several criminal complaints by one of the many firms that Jill's dad represented. I was flabbergasted!

"Jill's dad must know you are both staying on his property right now, right?" Cal stood up urgently.

"He wasn't there when we first arrived, but I'm sure at some point he would have been told by Vee or Walt that we were staying at the guesthouse. Do you know him? Do you think he'd do anything to Jill or Darcy? We need to get back over there now!"

I was starting to get frenzied with the thought that we'd put ourselves in even greater danger. During the trial, I hadn't connected the dots between Darcy, the club, and Chip's father. I was kicking myself for not doing any deeper due diligence than what appeared to apply directly to the case. I'd thought it was simple, not the easiest case, but simple on the facts. I wondered if I'd distracted myself with my dad's illness and perhaps didn't give my whole attention to the case, but I knew deep down that wasn't true. I'd wanted to win for so many reasons, but it hadn't worked out. I felt guilty for being blinded by my ambition.

"We need to get back over there and call Jill on our way to tell her what we found out and that she's not safe there." Cal started dialing her number.

"She's not going to answer. She never does, which drives me insane! I still need to find that file. Plug in a quick search for civil cases regarding the Maiden Voyage Club and print whatever comes up so we can tell who is a part of the corporation. I've met Jill's dad, and I can't imagine he'd ever hurt Jill or put her in danger." Cal looked at me hard when I said this because we needed to leave now, but I pointed to the computer. I was stressed about the girls, but I also knew this would be the only chance to get this information that might help us. Jill's dad's reputation in New Orleans was impeccable. He gave a ton of money to Tulane and it was hard to believe that kind of guy would be involved in anything shady. I needed some clear-cut evidence either way.

"Cal, you know her dad, what do you think about this? Do you have any idea what is going on?" Cal was on the phone and typing into the computer to pull up the information I wanted, so I ran over to the file cabinet and quickly grabbed a few files I thought might be relevant and then hustled to get the key back to the desk of Bruce's secretary. Cal came walking toward me from the printer.

"Damn it, right to voicemail." He turned away from me, and I could still hear him leaving a very short "call me now" message and hung up. He snatched up a handful of pages. "OK, here it is. You can read it to me on the way over. Let's get out of here."

We hurried down the stairs and Cal told me how he'd heard a little bit about the Maiden Voyage Club situation because he'd been helping the FBI as part of a liaison project with the Jefferson police. They were working together on a corruption operation against the NOPD. It was a project that not too many officers wanted to get involved with—for obvious reasons. "They've been pushing me hard to come onboard full-time. It's on the down low, so please don't blow it for me by saying anything. I'd help you guys as a friend anyhow. Jill is like a sister to me, and I'd never want to see any harm come to either of you."

I felt very alert even though I hadn't slept. With Cal here, I had confidence that I would be safe and that we would figure out who was at the bottom of all of this. There was so much rumor of corruption in the force it felt good that we could investigate privately.

"Listen, I know Jill's dad too. He can be a pompous asshole at times, especially to Jill, but he still can be a good guy. He fights for what he wants, kind of like someone we both know. I do believe there must be some explanation for all of this. Though, I'm not going to lie to you, I am concerned about you and Darcy being in the middle of this. It's not safe."

I'd never told Jill, but at the DA's office we often talked about the various defense lawyers, and Jill's dad consistently came up. I thought that either someone was using him or he was corrupt but hid it well. I couldn't wait to dig into the files.

"Let's call Walt and have him go over to the guesthouse to make sure Jill and Darcy are okay." It was nearly daylight.

As we came outside the DA's office, the sun was starting to come up over the buildings and out of the corner of my eye I saw one of the security guards amble from his car and head into the building's main door. Although it probably wouldn't have mattered, I didn't want anyone questioning me about being in the building. I didn't know if anyone knew I had returned from New York, and I certainly didn't want anyone to notice some of the files I'd taken. We got into the car and I started flipping through the files. Cal called Walt and left a message for him to call us as soon as he could and that it was urgent.

"Doesn't anyone pick up their phone anymore?" Cal accelerated and my head jerked back against the seat. He reached out and put his hand on my shoulder. "Sorry about that. Tell me what the files say. Need me to turn on the light?"

I could read the file clearly enough in the morning light. I wasn't sure exactly what I was looking for, so I started with lawyers involved. The name of Maurice Lejeune, Jill's dad, was on every case in which the Maiden Voyage Club was involved. Dick Hebert, Chip's dad, was attached to each corporate matter whether it was the club or something else. Could this have been the person Jill's dad said he regretted being involved with?

I started thinking that Jill's dad had more of a connection to my case with Darcy but I needed to dig a bit more to find out exactly what it was. I flipped through the pages of the files and tried to make note of anything remotely related.

When we pulled onto Jill's street there were cars parked on each side, a few of which had been there the night before. I ran over to the door, but it was locked.

"Damn it, I've locked us out!" I fiddled with the lock like Jill had done.

"I think I might still have a key," Cal said, which surprised me. He reached in his pocket and pulled out a different key chain than his car keys. He tried one that didn't work, but then the second one did. I was a little weirded out by this since Walt said he hadn't seen Cal in a while, but I didn't have time to ask Cal because I rushed immediately over to the guesthouse. It was quiet except for the crickets. Jill was infamous for oversleeping. We'd set the alarm, but it wouldn't be going off for at least another hour or two. I rushed up the stairs. I didn't care if I was pounding like an elephant. I entered Jill's room first since her light was on even though I remember turning it off when I left to meet Cal. She wasn't in bed, but the bathroom door was closed.

"Jill, Jill, you in there?" I knocked on the door. When she didn't answer, I turned the lock. The medicine cabinet was open and a wet towel was on the floor, but she wasn't there. I ran across the hall to Darcy's room and she wasn't there either. I looked out the window and saw Cal running over to Walt, who was over by the garage. Aside from some ruffled bed covers, the house looked the same as when I'd left. Where would they go at this hour? I ran downstairs and over to Cal and Walt, who were talking over by the garage.

"They're going to be fine." Walt was calm and acting like this was just any other day.

"Where did they go? And who did they go with? There's no note or anything over there." I was huffing a bit from running over from the guesthouse.

"They went to the Lejeune's plantation house up in Clinton," Walt said as if I should know exactly where that was and what that meant.

"Where the hell is Clinton and who did they go with?"

"Abby, calm down, calm down. They're okay. Mr. and Mrs. Lejeune took the girls up to his granddaddy's old plantation house. It's less than an hour outside of Baton Rouge. It used to be a cotton plantation, but now it's a place they go to relax or to escape when there's a flood warning." Walt told us this as if it was the most normal thing in the world to drive two hours out of town at the crack of dawn with no reasonable explanation, as if it were a family trip.

"Did they tell you why they were going up there? Did the girls want to go? Listen, I don't care what kind of place it is. Cal, we must go up there! What is going on?" My phone started ringing and I jumped. I dug into my bag, hoping it was Jill giving me an explanation, but it wasn't. It was my mother. I turned off the phone and shoved it back in my bag. I didn't have time for her now, not during all of this.

"Abby, come on. We've got to go."

"Are we going to Clinton?"

"I am going up there now and will call you when I get there. I know a few people up there so I'll have backup if I need it. It's not safe for both of us to be there. You need to stay here and get to Hibernia Bank when it opens and get into that lockbox of Darcy's." Cal handed me an envelope. "Walt gave me this. He said that Jill gave it to him before she left." I looked inside: there was a key, Darcy's ID, and a note.

"What does it say?" Cal asked.

"It says for me to go to Hibernia to get the documents. They are okay and will call."

"Well, that means I need to follow them. I don't trust that. He could have told her to write anything."

"I wonder why he didn't wait and try to get the documents for himself?" I said.

"I'll tell you how to get to the house. Lots of wide-open space up there. It's a little tricky finding which house since the signage is a little crazy," Walt said.

"Oh, I'll be able to find it. I've been up there a few times." Cal was nonchalant when he said this.

"When had you been up there, Cal?" It was hard to keep track of all the family connections at Jill's house.

"I've gone up a few times for some of the reunions."

"Reunions? What kind of reunion is held up there?"

"Well, Mr. Lejeune holds a reunion every few years for the descendants of the slaves his ancestors used to own. My mother is the great-great-granddaughter of one of them. Jill's dad is one of the main proponents for reparations to the slave families up in Clinton. I don't like to talk about it too much, but he even paid for my law school education. That's part of what he does and the reason for the reunions."

I'd never heard of anything like this, especially being from the North. "That's pretty incredible. And um…I didn't realize you went to law school too?"

"Make sure you get to Hibernia when it opens. I'm going to get on my way and will call you when I get there. I hope to get up there, talk to them, and be back by noon. I'll only feel good once I know that Jill is okay. Call me as soon as you find out anything."

"I will Cal, I promise." And he headed out. I asked Walt if I could go in the main house and use the computer. He brought me to Mr. Lejeune's office and turned on the computer. As soon as he left the room, I couldn't help myself. I had to see what he had in his computer about the Maiden Voyage Club. Also, I wanted to see if there was any evidence that he had known Darcy or Dick Hebert. There had to be something connecting everyone.

Now, I finally had the time to find the connection without sneaking around. His computer booted up, and I saw a link to "Current Cases." I clicked and went down the list of files. I was surprised that it wasn't password-protected. "Bingo," I thought to myself, and clicked on Maiden Voyage Club. What surprised me was within the club's folder there were smaller folders with names. There was one titled "Hebert, C.," and another link that said "Smith, D." I looked up to make sure that Walt wasn't near the room and clicked open the "Smith, D." file. As I was reading the file, I slowly began to understand *everything*.

CHAPTER 20

I printed the entire "Smith, D." file so I could continue reading it later. I did not want to make Walt suspicious that I was in Mr. Lejeune's office for too long—I'd only told him that I needed to get online for a little bit of research. There were so many different documents in the file I hadn't known where to start. But at least now I knew that Darcy Smith, Jill's dad, Chip's dad, and the Maiden Voyage Club were connected. I clicked on each folder and printed the entire thing.

Vee popped her head in the office and startled me: "Abby, you going to be working in here for a little bit? I heard what was going on. Can I bring you anything?"

"What did you hear, Vee?" I said and jerked up from the computer. The printer was making noise churning out the bulk of documents. If the proof was on any of those documents, I was going to find it.

"Well, Mr. Lejeune was very upset when he finally got home from Atlanta. Honestly, I thought you'd be with the girls when he went over to wake them up. He said everyone needed to go now, and that Walt and I shouldn't tell anyone where they had gone, except for you. The little note you scribbled that said you were with Cal assured them that at least *you* were okay. Thank goodness!"

"Did he say why they had to leave so quickly?" I asked.

"We weren't sure because it all happened in a frenzy. Mr. Lejeune seemed to know the other girl, but from the looks of it, Jill seemed very upset and didn't want to go. I don't know what he finally said to make her get in the car, but she finally did."

"Really? How did Jill's dad know Darcy?"

"Honestly, dear, and I know I'm speaking out of turn, but I knew that Mr. Lejeune had another child from an indiscretion a long time ago, but they never talked about it. I wouldn't be surprised if somehow this girl has something to do with that. It wouldn't be unlike him to send money or get a girl like that a job."

"I'm worried about Jill and Darcy. How can you be so sure that he's not going to hurt them?"

"I've been with this family a long time and one thing I know about Mr. Lejeune is that he prizes family. He would do anything to protect them."

"I'm confused, Vee. I don't know what is going on and why they had to leave. I wish someone would just give me some answers."

"You let me know if there is anything I can do to help." Vee headed back toward the kitchen.

"I only have a few more things to print, and I'll be out of here." As soon as Vee left the room, I tried Jill's cell phone again while the printer continued churning the pages. When her phone went to voicemail, I said, "Jill, call me. I need to talk to you." If she didn't pick up her messages soon, Jill was going to have a mailbox full of messages like that from both Cal and me. I was going to kill her if I got back to the guesthouse and found her cell in the room! I tried Cal and left a message for him to call me too. He was probably in a dead spot on the bayou.

I yawned and leaned back in Mr. Lejeune's big comfy office chair and tried to take in what Vee had told me. I was starting to feel a little groggy from waking up so early. I probably had at least fifty pages to print. My phone rang again—I picked up immediately and said, "Jill?"

"You called me, Abby, so I'm calling you back." It was Johnny. Ouch, his voice sounded like he was trying to be cold. For a second, I felt a heavy weight and wondered if I should say anything to him, but I was too busy to have this conversation now. I thought that he had a right to know, even if he hated me forever. "Johnny, I wanted to come clean with you and really apologize. I know after I tell you this you might never want to talk to me again."

"Jeez, Abby, stop being so overly dramatic—I'm sorry we left on such a sour note, but I've got to get going to work and I thought I might catch you before you went to work too."

"I wanted you to know the truth. I should have told you while I was there, but I was so happy to see you and felt like we still had a connection even after I abandoned you. Then, when I saw you and Jason arguing, I knew I couldn't let it go any further, and I had to tell you it was me."

"What do you mean?"

"I was the driver in the accident. It was all my fault. You were out cold. Jason switched us so I wouldn't get in trouble and you took all the blame." There was silence on the line when I said this. "Johnny, are you still there?" I winced as if he were going to reach through the phone and slap me.

"That's what you wanted to tell me?" His tone was much lighter than I anticipated. I started breathing quickly and then slowed myself by pushing out my exhale until my stomach was tight. Between this and the shit going on with Jill and Darcy, I was going to have a heart attack. "Jason is a manipulative asshole. I thought that before and I still think it now. That is one of the most ridiculous things I've ever heard. Do you believe everything you hear?"

"It's my fault, Johnny. I should have gone to jail, but I was too much of a coward to say anything." I felt the years of guilt start to bubble up, but it was such a relief to let it go.

The printer stopped and I looked at the pile of paper. I hoped I could find what I needed to get some answers. I thought I heard more people outside in the front of the house; I peered around, but didn't see anyone.

"Abby, I appreciate what you're doing here, I really do, but it's impossible. That guy has brainwashed you. Don't you think if I wasn't driving I would have said so?"

"I thought you were protecting me!" Now, I wondered if things had happened the way I thought they had happened or had I just listened to Jason and believed what he'd told me. I was getting nervous about taking too long in the office and not hearing from Jill or Cal. I couldn't believe that Darcy might be Jill's half-sister. It was all too much!

"You know, we never really had a chance, did we? Things got way too screwed up; the accident was the kicker. You passed out as soon as we got in the car. I shoved you over so I could drive since we didn't have far to go. Obviously, that was stupid. Neither one of us should have been driving. It's something that I'm going to regret for the rest of my life; I can never take it back. But know this: Jason is manipulative and would say or do anything to get you back. Why do you think we had that fight? Sometimes the truth is right in front of you and you need to trust that. Stop doubting yourself. You're an amazing person, and I wished things had turned out differently for us, but they didn't."

I thought I was going to cry when Johnny said this, but I didn't. I felt stronger. I thought about what he said about the truth. I was torn between wanting to talk to him and needing to go through the documents and figure out what was going on here.

"Johnny, I really hope we can at least be friends someday. I should have trusted you and given you more support. What can I say except I'm sorry for everything, mostly that I let you down by not being a friend."

"It was really a great surprise to see you again, Abby. I'm glad you called to tell me this. Now go take care of your shit. I know you must have something big going on or you wouldn't have rushed back. Just so you know, Jason has been hanging out at your mom's house."

"I'll be in touch, Johnny."

"Take care, Abby, and believe in yourself. I need to get my life together. I'll call you sometime, okay?" He hung up. That hurt a little because I knew that it was probably a nice way of breaking any ties between us. I felt empowered by coming clean with him, even though it made the hair on my arms stand up when he told me about Jason. I was ashamed I'd abandoned him because of the lies I believed from Jason, but I didn't have time to dwell on it.

Jill and Darcy could be in grave danger and I was wasting time! I scooped up the printed pages and started to read. The Hebert documents were on top and didn't seem to mean much at first. I skimmed through to get to the ones about Darcy. I couldn't imagine why there would be anything on her, since she was only a bookkeeper at the club, but since she'd lied to me I knew there had to be something I was missing.

When I stood up from the desk to head back over to the guesthouse to read over the pages, I saw Walt talking to two police officers. I gasped. I wondered if they were the same two who had come to my apartment and roughed up Jill. For a moment, I was glad that she wasn't here, but I wondered if she was in worse trouble up in Clinton at the plantation house. Then I realized: They were coming to find me! I ducked down below the windowsill. If they started to charge into the main house, I was going to have to find a way to escape. I wanted to look around, but I couldn't take my eyes off Walt and the cops. Where were they going? Why were they here? I felt paralyzed. Then I saw them shaking Walt's hand and walking out toward the front gate. Walt came back toward the house. I gathered the pages and took one last peek on the computer to see if I had missed any files. While I waited for the computer to shut down, I opened the drawers of the desk to find anything else that might be pertinent to the case. Then, I headed toward the door.

Walt came toward me. "Abby, we have to talk." When he said this, he was so calm, but I wondered what he had told the cops.

"What's going on?" I didn't want to tell him about seeing him talking to the policemen unless he mentioned it to me. I'd had such a good feeling about Walt when I'd met him, but I felt like my intuition was out of whack and I couldn't tell who I could trust.

"They were looking for Mr. Lejeune. I told them that he was still in Atlanta, which is what he wanted me to say. He also told me to help you. Cal told me that too. I haven't been sure what's going on since both you and Jill showed up. Maybe after the trip to the morgue with you two, I don't want to know. But I'll keep you safe."

"Thing is, Walt, I'm not completely sure either, that's part of the problem. I spoke to Vee inside, and she thinks that Darcy may be connected to the family, but the rest of them may not be privy to it. Not to mention that the Maiden Voyage Club is at the apex of it all."

"Abby, I've heard of the place, of course. I'll be honest, I also heard Mr. Lejeune mention a woman named Darcy. At the time, I didn't think anything of it or even attempt to connect the dots until you and Jill brought her over here with you the other night. When I told him you all were staying here, Mr. Lejeune was upset. He called me from Atlanta late last night and must've gotten the next flight. Once he arrived, he got everyone moving to get on up to the plantation."

"Did Jill resist?" I asked.

"He was making so much noise and she was going to put up a fight like she always does—you know those two don't get along so well—and then I went into the house to get a few things so I missed any argument. When I came back out, both girls were crying. Jill indicated that she was okay, so I didn't ask any questions. When those cops came here asking questions, I truly didn't know anything. But I knew enough not to tell them about the house in Clinton."

"Will they figure that out and go up there? I need to warn Cal!"

"I think they are going to search around New Orleans for a while longer. Not too many people outside the family know about the Clinton place. Mr. Lejeune values his privacy. You have time to get the information you need—which I'm guessing you were printing out in there. Tell me, how can I help?" Walt straightened his cap and pushed his glasses up over his nose. His face had those wrinkles that made him look very warm and worn.

"Well, I have to go over to the Hibernia Bank near St. Mary's in the Lower Garden District to pick up something in a lockbox."

"I can drive you over there—it'll be quicker."

"You sure you don't have anything else going on that you need to do?"

"I know I need to do something to help the Lejeune family, and particularly Jill. I need to help."

"Think they'll be open yet?"

"By the time we drive over there, we'll probably have to wait a few minutes. We can get you some coffee while you wait. You look like you need some."

"I didn't sleep too well last night with everything going on." I looked at the clock. "Let me read what I've printed out to see if I can find anything in there. Actually, I can read on the way."

"I'll grab the keys."

I stood out on the front porch and then sat down on the steps. It was already starting to get warm. I hoped if I got a little coffee in me I would get a second wind. I needed to figure out the connections before something bad happened to Jill or Darcy...or Cal for that matter. As I flipped through the pages of documents, all I could think about was Darcy's connection to all of it. Then I turned to the page that seemed to answer everything.

CHAPTER 21

•◦••━━●━━━━━●━━━━━●━━••◦•

Apparently, Mr. Lejeune had figured out from information provided to him by Darcy that the Maiden Voyage Club was engaged in illegal activities that went beyond money laundering from dummy corporations based in Harahan. One of the documents I found detailed a confrontation with Dick Hebert about withdrawing his representation, but that had resulted in Hebert threatening to harm both of his daughters. It seemed Darcy had confided in Chip that Mr. Lejeune was her father and had used his connections to get her job there.

"You ready to head on out, Abby?" Walt shouted and I nodded. I'd been sitting on the porch pouring through the pages. If anything, there was something to learn by Mr. Lejeune's copious note-taking. Every conversation, documentation, and observation was recorded.

Could it be that Mr. Lejeune tried to unravel himself from a psycho client and caused all of this? I thought that he was smarter than that. I hopped in the car with Walt so I could keep up the momentum. "Let's head up St. Charles. Can you drop me off at the bank—think it's best if I go in alone. And thanks for doing this, Walt."

"Not a problem," Walt said as cheerfully as ever.

When we rolled out onto the street, I looked around to make sure the two cops weren't around. I thought about asking Walt to keep watch for those cops, but then it would draw attention to something that seemed fishy. The street seemed still and the Quarter still quiet at this early hour. Walt turned on the radio to a local news station, and we cruised along.

"I'm going to try Cal again."

Cal picked up right away. "I'm almost there, Abby. What's going on there? Did you get to the bank yet or find out anything?" I told him about Mr. Lejeune, Darcy, and the Maiden Voyage Club connections along with the problems with Mr. Hebert. "Shit, now I've really gotten you in over your head, Abby. Who are you with now?"

"Walt is taking me over to the bank."

"Did Walt have any idea what was going on?" I wanted to tell Cal about the cops, but I didn't want to say anything in front of Walt. So, I said, "Absolutely, he does. We'll be fine here."

"What the heck do you mean by that?"

"No, Walt doesn't mind taking me over to the bank. Says he's got the time this morning, especially with Mr. Lejeune over at his office so early."

"Abby, you think Walt has something to do with this?" Finally, Cal caught on.

"Definitely, you got it," I said.

"I'm going to take care of things here and head back as fast as possible. I think you need to go straight in the front door of that bank, get the papers, and ask the bank manager to fax them. Call me back right before you step into the bank, and I'll give you the number. Right now, you just need to answer, 'Yes, sounds good,' and not say anything else right now, okay?" I still felt a bit uneasy, but relieved at least Cal would be able to help. I couldn't imagine Walt being involved, but at this point I was sure something was amiss.

"Sounds good, Cal."

"I'll call you soon."

"Okay, then…" I didn't know what else I was supposed to say.

"Cal get up there okay?" Walt said to me as he turned on to St. Charles.

"He's just about there," I replied, trying not to sound weird. I pointed at the bank: "It's right over there on the corner." Walt went past St. Mary's, so he could turn around over the streetcar tracks and drop me off right next to the building. "I'll be right back." I hopped out of the car and sprinted into the bank vestibule. It was quiet, and it looked like I might be the first customer of the day. I called Cal back and told him about the interaction I'd seen at the house: "Cal, what is going on? Is Walt involved?"

"Listen, Abby, I've known Walt all my life, but something about him talking to the cops and them leaving immediately doesn't seem right. I don't know how else all the information Mr. Lejeune was gathering could have been found out by Hebert unless someone leaked it." "But why would he do that?"

"Money. That would be the only thing. But listen, we don't have a lot of time. I need you to get the bank manager to fax some of those documents to my contacts over at the FBI. I've given them a heads-up on what was going down, and I don't want this to get any messier than it already is. I want you to be safe. I'll be back soon. Call me when you get back in the car." I found a pen in my bag and wrote the fax number on my hand.

I stepped inside the bank and went over to one of the men at the desks and told him I wanted to go into my safety deposit box. I'd seen this particular guy at the bank before but, since I only used the ATM, I'd had never had any direct dealings with him. If anyone was going to question me, it would be the woman with a permanent scowl on her face who I'd seen there before. So, I decided it was best to pick the guy that looked the most inexperienced and sweet-talk him if he asked any questions about my ID. He didn't. I put my ID on the table, scribbled a signature, and he led me to the security boxes. When I opened the box, I found only one manila envelope. I sat down at the small table in the room and emptied the contents. In it were all the provision sheets from the operation in Harahan that detailed the "packages" brought over from Poland, along with some accounting sheets that I'm sure had the details for some of the dummy businesses. At the bottom of each sheet was Dick Hebert's signature, which was the proof I needed.

"Do you think I could pay to fax a few pages of this over to my office before I leave? I work at the DA's office," I added, thinking that would add a little credibility to my request.

"How many pages?" the clerk asked, who was not unfriendly, but acted as if he might be doing me a big favor.

"About twenty," I said thinking that would be enough to give them some solid information to go on without taking too much time.

"Dollar a page," he said and winked. I wasn't sure if he was being cute or obnoxious.

"That's fine," I said and followed him back to his desk. I handed him the pages and the fax number. Luckily, I still had about forty dollars left in my wallet, so I gave him one of the twenties. He took it and put it into his drawer; I looked away. My phone rang again. This time, it was Jill.

"Abby, I'm so glad you answered. Are you okay?" Jill sounded exasperated.

"I'm okay, Jill. What about you…what's going on? Are you?" I spoke softly since I did not want to make a big scene and felt rude talking on my cell in the bank.

"It's kind of a crazy story. I'm sorry we left you there, but Dad said you'd be okay if you were with Cal."

"Vee told me that Darcy is your sister. Is that true?"

"I can't even talk about that right now, I'm so pissed. Once Dick Hebert got a whiff of that, he knew he could get my father to do whatever he wanted if he threatened to harm his girls. He must have had his goons somehow track me down to your apartment. They wanted to send my dad a message. You know, I think he's an asshole most of the time, but Dad wanted to get us out of there to keep us safe. Why don't you come out here too?"

"Well, I think Clinton is a little far—I think I'll take my chances here."

"Clinton? Why would we be up at the plantation? We're at my aunt's house in Metairie. Dad thought it was best to get off the property in case someone came around to question us. He went to the office and is going to try to get Darcy's documents out of the safety deposit box with an affidavit."

"Jill, Walt told me you were in Clinton, so Cal headed up there to go help you. We weren't sure how your dad was involved. I'm at the bank getting the documents that Darcy put in the safety deposit box."

"Why would Walt say that? He suggested Clinton, but we told him that was too far and figured staying in Metairie would be fine. It's not like we need to be in witness protection or anything. Jesus, do you think Walt could be involved?"

"Listen, Jill, let me call you back. I've got to get out of here, and Walt is waiting for me outside. I've got to see if I can get out another way. I'll call you."

"Be careful, Abby. Maybe you should go back with him and pretend there was nothing in the box." That wasn't a bad idea except, since I knew that Jill had been roughed up by the two cops, I couldn't be sure that Walt hadn't told them where we were. In that case, they might be waiting for me once I stepped outside the bank.

"I think I have a plan. I'll call you." As soon as I hung up, I texted Cal that Jill was in Metairie and to turn around right away. I watched as Jerry—I'd caught his name tag—stood shrugged over the fax machine as if in his own world. I grabbed a small stack of account applications off his desk and put them into the manila folder. Then I stood up and walked to the middle of the bank so I could see outside the main doors. Walt was still on the street with the car idling. My mind started racing about what I should do. I knew there wasn't a back entrance to the bank. I was also sure *if* there were a bathroom I could use, the window would definitely be hooked up to an alarm system. I decided to take my chances and give Walt a bullshit story that I had to go up to my apartment to get some of my notes on the case. Surely, he wouldn't argue with that.

Jerry came back after faxing the documents and handed them to me.

"I know this is asking a huge favor of you, but could you fax them once more?" I was pushing my luck, but thought if I could get these papers to Jill's dad with a note on top about Walt's involvement, then I'd feel like I'd accomplished something.

"I don't see why not." I reached in my bag to give him another twenty. Someone who was probably his manager walked by and waved his hand at me. "It's a silly rule. I'm sure I can let this one fly, but next time, let's think about scanning, okay?"

"Mind if I do a quick search on your computer?" I was pushing it, but I needed to make sure I got Mr. Lejeune's right number. Jerry scooted over and handed me a post-it. I wasn't sure exactly what to write to Mr. Lejeune so that the message would be helpful but not too revealing to whoever picked up the fax. I told him briefly that Walt was involved, I had the documents, and I needed him to act as soon as possible. I hoped that was enough because I was nervous about what would happen.

While Jerry was still faxing, I stood to leave but he caught me and said, "Don't you want your documents?"

"Thanks for your help." I grabbed the documents. On my way out, I put the manila folder under my arm and unsure what to do with the real documents, I stopped near the deposit slip area and threw the whole bunch of documents into the trash. I had to trust that the copies I sent would be enough. After all, they weren't originals in the first place. Darcy had copied them from the originals.

I stepped outside and saw that Walt was talking to one of the cops who looked like he had been at the house. The hair on the back of my neck stood up. I waved to Walt with one finger to indicate that I'd forgotten something in the bank. The cop looked at me and then at Walt. Although part of me wanted to run, I walked back inside the bank, took the documents out of the garbage, shoved them into the folder, and beelined it for Jerry.

"Jerry, I'm sorry, is there a bathroom in here? I'm not going to make it if I leave without going," I said with a smile. Jerry got up and I followed him. I prayed that there was a window in the bathroom. I didn't care if there was an alarm—maybe that would be a good thing—because I didn't want to find out what Walt and that cop had in mind for me.

CHAPTER 22

T he window in the bathroom wouldn't budge. I contemplated breaking it—there had to be another way out of the bank aside from the front door! I didn't have much time before Walt got suspicious and came to find me inside. I decided that I would have to go out the front door and take my chances. After flushing the toilet and running the water in the sink, I exited the bathroom, returned to the lobby of the bank, and headed for the front door. Jerry waved to me and I waved back.

As I hit the front door to the vestibule, I saw Walt pulling away. Now, there was a different cop there, who must have tried to write Walt a ticket for no parking, which made him go around the block again. This was my chance, so I made a run for it, hoping that the time it took for Walt to maneuver around the block would give me time to get to the front door of my apartment without him seeing me. As soon as I rounded the corner, I could see my well-worn, light-pink building sandwiched between the washed-out, baby blue building and the yellow three-story one. I ran as fast as I could across the road, up the sidewalk, and made it up the brick stairs just as Walt was turning the corner. I reached inside my bag for my keys and stood frozen inside the vestibule of the doorway, holding my breath and waiting to see if his car stopped. It didn't.

I rushed upstairs to Candice's apartment and knocked hard. I felt bad waking her up because I knew she always got home well after three from Molly's, the dive bar she bartended at in the Quarter. I was tempted to run across the hall to check out my apartment, but didn't want to waste any time.

Candice came to the door in her clothes from the night before and raccoon eyes from her makeup. "What?" was all she could muster when she saw me.

"I'm really sorry, Candice. I'm desperate right now. Can I use your car?"

Candice stepped back in her apartment without saying a word. She came back, handed me the keys and said, "Prytania Street on the right, you'll see it."

"Thanks, Candice, I'll have it back to you in a few hours." Although I wouldn't consider Candice a good friend, we'd shared a few drinks together on our fire escapes and picked up each other's mail when necessary. I'd borrowed her car once before when mine was in the shop after our street had flooded from some heavy rains. She didn't mind, and she never asked any questions. Whenever I asked her something about herself, she poured me another drink.

"Don't worry about it," she said, hardly opening her eyes.

I was heading downstairs when I heard someone fumbling with the front door—I ran back up before Candice had locked her door. I pushed her door open and said, "Fire escape! Don't tell anyone you saw me!" I could see evidence on her coffee table that she had never gone to sleep after coming home from Molly's. There was a mirror on her coffee table next to an open bottle of wine and a wine glass. The room smelled like incense. I ran over to her window, which was large due to the cathedral ceiling rooms, and got out on the fire escape. I motioned for her to close the window and shut the curtains.

I'd only sat on the fire escape, but never jumped down from it. I looked for some clips to release the ladder because there was no way I could jump from where I was and not get hurt. I found the clips and as soon as I released them, the ladder rushed down and nearly touched the ground. I started climbing down. When I glanced up, I could see that Candice had closed the curtains. I wiped my brow before I went under the platform and started climbing down. When I got to the bottom, I hung for a second and then released my hands and touched the ground.

I looked around at the potted plants on the back patio near the laundry area. It was quiet back here and private. I headed around to the left side of the building over by the laundry room to see if I could see Walt's car out in front. I pushed myself through the neighbors' bushes, jumped over the low fence and started running through front lawns until I rounded the corner to Prytania. I looked back and didn't see Walt or the cop. I panicked for a second when I didn't see Candice's car, but it was tucked in front of a big black SUV. Her car was hard to miss because it was an old VW Beetle that she had hand-painted a variety of colors. It was a cool but crazy little car; I prayed that it started. I put the key in and it choked for a second, but then it purred that familiar Beetle sound. I pulled out and felt a wave of relief. I headed uptown, although I didn't know where I should go or what I was going to do except call Cal.

"Did you get my text? When will you get here Cal? There is some serious shit going on. I don't know what's up with Walt, but I'm scared and not sure what to do."

"Abby, Abby, calm down. I'm on my way back. Where are you now?"

"I'm headed uptown. I have a friend's car. Did you hear me? Walt is definitely involved in whatever is going on around here!"

"That's interesting," he said with concern.

"Walt was talking with one of those bad cops. I faxed the documents to that number you gave me and to Mr. Lejeune's office; I kept a copy instead of chucking them just to be safe." I told Cal about how I ditched Walt and how the cop had most likely figured out that I went to my apartment.

"Are you okay, Abby?"

"Where should I meet you?"

"I'm headed over to Harahan. Why don't you meet me over there in the Kmart parking lot? It's not too far from the office."

"You're not going over there by yourself, are you?"

"We need to make sure we get to the office space before they shut it down on us. My department is working together with the FBI at this point. I let them know what was going on last night, but we knew we had to act quickly. From what I can gather, we probably don't have more than a few hours. I should be there in an hour. Do you want to stop to write down the directions Jill gave me?"

"Give me some landmarks." I turned on to Carrolton to make my way over to Jefferson on 90. He described what seemed like an easy way to get to the dummy offices. I was sure I wouldn't have any trouble finding them; but, I felt a little scared. "Are a lot of cops going to be there? Walt might figure things out and follow me."

"Don't worry, Abby. If he does, that's good. I'll take care of things and see you there."

"I'm driving a little painted VW Beetle. You can't miss me," I said. I felt ridiculous driving it. However, I'd narrowly escaped a bad situation. Somehow, in driving this obtrusively painted car, I had become incognito.

I was feeling like I had been hit by a truck, so when I came up to Maple Street I turned. I desperately needed to make a quick detour for an iced coffee at PJ's. My adrenaline was about to crash. It was hard to believe that Walt was somehow involved. It was going to crush Jill. I parked the Beetle, and dashed into PJ's to order my usual.

"Hey, Abby!" I spun around because it sounded an awful lot like Jason. "Aren't you Jill's friend?" The man was bohemian-looking and definitely *not* Jason, but I couldn't figure out who he was or when I had met him before.

"Yeah, I know Jill. Have we met?" Since this was Jill's neighborhood and coffee haunt, it wasn't surprising that I'd bump into someone she knew, but I didn't have time to engage. I was about third in line and hoped they'd get to me quickly so I could get out of there and get to Harahan. I had only stopped because I couldn't keep my eyes open.

"We met briefly at the Maple Leaf Bar one night. I think Rockin' Dopsie Jr. was playing."

"Oh, probably so…." There was a good likelihood that I was drunk, so there was a slim chance I would remember meeting him. With his Birkenstock sandals, he looked like he was a philosophy student, definitely someone Jill would befriend. It was finally my turn, so I ordered a large flavored iced coffee with milk.

"How's Jill? I haven't seen her in a while. Still up to her same old shit?" His arm brushed against mine.

"Same old shit, you know." That was sort of the truth, but certainly not any indication of what we'd gone through in the past few days. The girl at the counter handed me my coffee. I gave her a few bucks and didn't wait for the change. "See ya," I said with a wave. As quickly as I could, I headed to the door before he could ask me anything else. But I froze when I got there. A cop car was driving by and slowed down by Candice's bug. That freaked me out. I thought about asking the guy for a ride to Harahan. As I walked back, he was walking out. "Can you do me a favor? I don't think my car is going to start. Could you give it a go for me?"

"Like I have the magic touch?" He raised his eyebrows to me.

"Something like that. With the kind of day I'm having so far, I could use a little break." I knew it was kind of an odd request, but it seemed like the cop was hovering at my car—waiting for me. I couldn't be sure Candice hadn't been forced to say something, but at least she didn't know where I was going. Maybe my paranoia was getting the best of me, but I couldn't afford to take any chances. I was stupid to have stopped in the first place, but I was fading, and I wasn't sure I could drive anymore without shutting my eyes. I handed him the keys and said, "I really appreciate it. I'm borrowing this crazy car, and it's driving me nuts."

"Why is that cop hovering? Your car doesn't have any tickets on it, does it?"

I shook my head.

"I'll see what I can do." I watched him walk over to the car. I tensed up because the cop was watching carefully, but once he got into the car, the cop drove away. Must have been a fluke. I walked over to the driver's side as he started the car up. It coughed a few times, and then started up and purred.

"Awesome! Thanks for doing this."

"You want to meet for coffee some day when you have more time?" I noticed a tiny ring in his nose that I hadn't noticed before. It was a mini bull-ring, and I found myself staring.

"Sure, just ask Jill for my number. I'm so late, I have to go." I felt flattered that a bohemian guy like that would be interested in someone like me.

"What's your name?"

"Abby Callahan," I said. I thought for a second about telling him that I was Candice, since I was driving her car and not feeling like myself today. But it didn't matter either way because he probably wasn't going to call.

I swung the car around to get back on Carrollton and make it to Jefferson Highway. As I drove, I thought about my dad and what he would have told me to do in a situation like this. I remembered the day he taught me to catch a football. He threw it over and over again until my hands got sore from practicing. I was also getting tired, but I was determined to learn how to catch the ball right. I was never going to be a great football player, but I was tough, which is what my dad said to me after we stopped throwing. I knew then, and I know now, that I just don't give up. I felt like this was one of those days. Obstacle after obstacle, I told myself to hold it together and be tough—rely on myself, trust my instincts. Everyone involved had something to gain, even Cal.

Johnny was right. I needed to watch out for myself and to be careful who I trusted.

CHAPTER 23

S omething about meeting Cal in a parking lot in Harahan before he made a bust didn't sit right with me. I had a strange feeling. Instead of going directly to Harahan, I scanned around for a safe place to pull over and park. I was going to call the FBI myself. I was starting to feel as if the only person I could trust was myself. I saw a Rally's on the next corner after the light and figured that was as good a place as any. Normally, I only considered it drunk food, like the time I forced Jill to eat greasy fries so she would make herself throw up. But, no one would notice me there, so it would be a good spot.

From our time at the morgue, I still had Doctor Mackinaw's card in my bag. He might be the one person who could direct me to an agent over at the FBI. Besides, he had told me to call. I didn't know what I'd tell him I was doing, but it didn't matter. I left him a message telling him to call me please. I hope he did for a few reasons. He was weird, but I liked him, and I'd probably make it down to the morgue again, so it would be nice to have a friend.

I made a few calls to the morgue and finally got someone to give me the number to the local FBI. I was surprised when someone answered the phone. I stuttered, "Um, uh, this is Abby Callahan. I have some information related to the Maiden Voyage Club and Dick Hebert. I'm about to meet a cop to hand off the documentation I've recovered from a sort of informant. I'm under the impression that the documentation has already been received by your office."

"What did you say your name was again, Miss?" The man who answered had a deep baritone voice and sounded helpful rather than accusatory.

"Abigail Callahan. I work at the DA's office." I managed to regroup, grasping for some additional credibility.

"Please don't hang up the phone. I'm going to transfer you to the agent handling that case."

"I'll wait." I felt relieved that someone was assigned to the "case" and considered hanging up and going to meet Cal promptly, but surely, I was being recorded and who knows what I'd find out. I looked around at the parking lot I'd pulled into. There weren't too many cars in the lot. I guess Rally's didn't do a big breakfast business. I was tempted to go get something, but I didn't want to take the chance of losing the connection. I could eat something later.

"This is Phil Landry," a voice said. He sounded about my age. I don't know why, but I pictured him in a suit and with red hair, kind of like a young Ron Howard. "Am I to understand that you have some documentation related to the Maiden Voyage Club?"

"Sir, I do." I explained what had transpired over the past twelve hours.

He listened and didn't give me any feedback except for a few "uh-hums" and "okays." I couldn't have been talking for more than a few minutes when Phil said, "Abby, where are you now?"

"I'm in the parking lot of a Rally's on Jefferson Highway, pretty close to the Huey Long Bridge." A car pulled into the lot and startled me until it went by and pulled up to the drive-through. I was jumpy.

"I'm really glad you called, and I'm going to need your help. Do you think you can stall your meet with Calvin for a good fifteen minutes? That's what I'm going to need to get over your way."

"Can you tell me what's going on? I've gotta admit I'm nervous about hanging out here. I borrowed my friend's car, and I feel a little exposed, although I don't know or understand who'd be following me unless these documents are even more important or valuable than I think they are...." I jumped again as another car pulled into the lot and drove around. Everyone who went by stared at Candice's Bug—I wasn't used to everyone gawking.

"I'll tell you more when I get there, but an officer named Cal or Calvin with the Jefferson Police is not working with our office. I'm not sure how you've gotten yourself involved in this, but your instinct was right to call. I'll be there in fifteen—stay put. And here's my cell phone if you need to reach me before I get there. Do you have a pen?"

"Hang on, and let me get a pen...." I dug into my bag and wrote his number on a paper bag that I had found on the floor of the car.

"I'll be there soon, Abby. Don't worry, everything will be fine." I put the bag down in the passenger seat and brought my hands up to my mouth and started breathing into them so I wouldn't hyperventilate. I was tempted to use the bag, but it was ripped and a little dirty. It was hard to believe that Cal was somehow involved in something. Was I so naive that everyone took me for a fool? I was trying to work out how he might be involved, but it was all so confusing! I couldn't believe that maybe I had put Darcy in danger again! But, as of right now, Cal didn't know where Darcy was so she was safe. I wanted to call Jill and tell her, but she probably wouldn't believe me, and Phil had advised me not to call anyone.

When my phone rang, I jumped. I hoped it was the FBI guy telling me that he'd taken care of everything. Instead, it was my mother again. If I picked her call up, I doubted Mom would have any good news, but it was too early for her to have gotten into any real trouble, so I picked it up anyhow. Hearing her voice was like a dose of her crazy reality.

"Abby, dear, how are you doing?" The rapid pace of her cadence concerned me.

"I'm okay, Mom. How are things there? I'm sorry I had to leave so abruptly," I said. I wished we'd been able to spend some time together when I wasn't feeling pissed off at her. I hated myself for feeling like that, but couldn't help it because when she took bunches of pills and booze she wasn't herself. I found her embarrassing and nonsensical.

"It's probably better that you did go, no use staying around here during these dreary times. I'm looking to get away myself." She surprised me. She hadn't gone away from home in years.

"Where would you go, Mom?"

"Well, if it wouldn't be too imposing, I thought I might come visit you. I know you've been annoyed by me for a while now, and you know, with your father gone, I'd like to see if I can fix that." I was completely taken aback.

"I'd like that. Tell me when and I'll take some time off work." I didn't know if she could do it, but I wanted to believe that she would come.

"You know, Abby, Jason came over the other night and said he wanted to talk to me about you."

"What'd you say?"

"I told him to take a hike. If you are finished with him, then why do I need to have a conversation with him? I'm sorry, but I never liked him. Something wasn't right about him. Your father always stuck up for him, but I kept my mouth shut. I just wanted you to be happy."

I was jolted by the knock on my window and screamed. Thank goodness Phil had his badge out. I hadn't noticed his black town car had pulled up on my passenger side.

"Abby?"

"Sorry, I have to go now, Mom. But let me know when you're

coming. That would be great. I'd really like the idea." For the first time, I meant it.

"I love you, Abby." She hung up before I had a chance to respond.

Phil put his ID away, and I got out of the car to talk to him. I looked around to see that more cars were pouring into the lot, but most of them were going to the drive-through.

"Phil Landry…you must be Abby. Why don't we go inside for a minute and sit down and talk?" He didn't look like Ron Howard at all. He was dark-haired and husky, about forty years old and wearing a nondescript blue suit. He looked like he'd been around for a long time, which made me feel at ease.

I grabbed my yellow messenger bag and followed him inside. Aside from two grey-haired men who were sitting in one of the booths drinking coffee and playing checkers, the place was quiet. We walked up to the front and he looked at me and said, "Coffee?"

"Iced." We stood at the front counter while the girl made our drinks.

"Okay, I know we don't really have a lot of time. There are a few other cars on the way. We didn't plan on blowing this thing wide-open today, but it looks like we have no choice. You've given us the link we were looking for. We didn't know who was providing the information between the U.S. Customs officers and the club. We knew it had to be a cop, but we couldn't figure out whom until we got your call. Can I look at the documents?"

I reached in my bag and gave him the manila folder with the documents. "What about my friends, Jill and Darcy? They could be in danger if Cal really is a bad guy."

"Do you know where they are staying? Does Cal?"

"Jill told me they were in Metairie at her aunt's house, but she didn't give me an address. I can call her."

"Let's wait a minute here. First, is this the Calvin you've been referring to?" He showed me a picture of Cal in his police uniform.

I nodded and shook my head. "As for your friends, Jill and Darcy, they'll be okay; I'm going to send someone over there to take care of them. I've also sent someone to Maurice Lejeune's office. Seems like his political ambitions have clouded his version of right and wrong. He is part of a conglomerate that had been funding this illegal operation from the start."

"Along with Dick Hebert?" I asked.

"Listen, I've already said too much. What I need you to do is to keep your meet with Cal, hand him the documents and go with him while he attempts to dismantle the office in Harahan. Do you think you can handle that? I don't think he wants to hurt you. You know enough, but you don't know how he's involved, so he has no reason to do anything to you. After all, you have what he wants."

"What if he changes his mind on that? I'm kinda scared of what he might do."

"I'm going to be following you and we have someone on the inside, so I won't let that happen."

"Cal told me that the girl on the inside was killed. I saw her when I went to the morgue. Her name was Nola. She was one of the girls killed in Louis Armstrong Park."

"That is unfortunately true, but she wasn't the only person we had working this case. It's been going on for several years. Your zealousness with Darcy's case somehow upset the whole apple cart. We think Maurice Lejeune was fine with most of the illegal operations. In fact, they were making him a lot of money, and he was also going to use them for political influence when he ran for office. But when it came down to smuggling the girls, he finally drew the line of decency. Of course, using his once estranged daughter to get the documentation to squeeze out Dick Hebert was ingenious and nearly foolproof. It was really tragic that both of those girls from the ship were killed."

"I don't understand why Cal would be involved." With the

opportunity given to him by Mr. Lejeune, I wondered how he could toss that away for money.

"We have to get moving. If you don't get to your meeting soon, he's going to think something is up. Do you think you can handle this?"

"I don't want anyone else getting hurt." I stood up to head out to my car. I knew there was always a choice, but I felt compelled to find the underlying cause of this. If Cal was a dirty cop, I was going to help Phil nail him and whomever else was involved.

CHAPTER 24

— • — • — • —

"**W**here the hell are you, Abby?" Cal sounded irate when I answered the phone after pulling out of Rally's with Phil on my tail.

"Almost there, Cal. Sorry, I get a little confused driving out here," I said, which was generally true anytime I ventured outside of Orleans Parish. I was completely spun around anytime I hopped off the I-10, unless I was going to the airport.

"We're a little crunched for time....Oh, there I see you now. What the hell are you driving?" he said and hung up. How could he have missed me? Candice's car was an eyesore.

I looked in my rearview mirror to check and see if Phil was still following me. He was, but he was far enough back that it didn't look like it. The area where I was meeting Cal was a little isolated, which made me slightly uncomfortable, especially knowing that Cal was dangerous and using me.

"Hey!" I hopped out of the car when I saw him.

"Jesus, Abby, what the hell happened? Are you okay?" Cal gave me a hug. I hoped he didn't feel me stiffen up. I tried to act normal.

"I don't know, Cal. I got a bad feeling about Walt when I saw him talking to the cops. I can't even believe that I gave him the slip."

"I'm sure he can't believe it either. I'm sure Mr. Lejeune told him to keep an eye on you for him."

"What do we need to do? And where are the FBI agents you were talking about?" I asked, even though I knew the answer. I pretended the plan was still the same. At least that's one good thing that came out of being with Jason: I'd gotten good at burying my feelings. It wasn't that hard putting on a poker face and faking that Cal was still a good guy.

"Listen, why don't you leave that car here and hop in with me," he said.

"I can't leave it. It's not my car. Candice would kill me if something happened to it."

"What are you worried about? I'll bring you back here when we're finished."

I didn't want to be without my own transportation. Not to mention, if Phil was following me, I was going to be much easier to spot in Candice's car. For all its ridiculousness, it was making me feel safe. "I won't leave the car around here. If there's not going to be anyone over at the offices, why does it matter?" I didn't care if I was being difficult; I wasn't going to leave the car.

"Abby, it's a Walmart parking area. Just get in the goddamned car and stop being difficult." He said this with a smile, but I knew he was being serious. I stared at him and looked around to see if there was anyone who might see me.

I moved around to the passenger side of his car and realized I'd forgotten my phone in the car. I must have dropped it so I jumped back out to get it. I hoped this little mishap had given Phil some extra time to do what he needed to do. I hopped back in Cal's car. My phone rang. When I answered it, I was a little surprised to see a number I didn't recognize, but the voice was a distinct pitch, which I recognized. "Hey, Doctor Mackinaw, thanks for ringing me back."

"Abby, I'm glad you called. I have some news and wasn't exactly sure how to reach you over the weekend."

Cal mouthed, "Who's that?"

"My doctor," I said, putting my hand over the phone. That was all he needed to know and that seemed to appease him as he started fiddling with his own cell phone. "What's going on?"

"That girl that your friend identified might be someone different. From what I can tell, this woman may also have been traveling with the other girl from Poland on that container ship you described. I need more evidence to prove it and was hoping you could help with that. Can you come down to my office? I'm off for lunch in a bit. If you're close, you can stop by."

"Let me see what I can do. I'll call you back soon."

"Abby, are you local? The police are on it already...." I didn't hear the rest of what he said because Cal was glaring at me and I had to hang up.

I hoped that Doctor Mackinaw didn't decide to get too involved. What he said about that girl not being Nola made me gravely concerned about my faith in Jill. I had let Jill into my home and my life. I couldn't believe she would use me like this. She had to be acting on the impetus of her father. I thought back to what had transpired since I'd left for New York after the trial. She'd been in my apartment, used my car, and had access to my things. And when Darcy came by to see me, she'd been at the door. Why hadn't she called me through all of this? Was the stint in the hospital a set-up? She'd seemed genuinely afraid, but maybe it was some kind of act?

"What's going on?" Cal said, zapping me back to the present.

"I'm worried about Darcy and Jill. I can't stop thinking that they're in danger. What if Mr. Lejeune hurts them? Or someone else?" As I said this, I looked around and it looked like we were going into some sort of warehouse area. I should have paid more attention. I had no idea where I was. I hoped to God that Phil was still behind us. I racked my brain on how I'd defend myself or what fib I could tell Cal to get myself out of here.

"You'll see them soon enough, no need to freak out." He slowed down and turned into an area that the yellow signage indicated was a dead end.

"Cal, where are we going? This doesn't seem like it leads to any working office," I said.

"Abby, you really shouldn't have gotten involved with this but here we are. Listen carefully, whatever happens, you are a conspirator and could be implicated in a crime."

"What are you talking about, Cal? I gave the information to you, you're a cop."

"We've got to dismantle what we have here and start fresh."

"Cal, can we talk about this? I can help you, nobody has to know what's going on, not even Jill," I lied. I didn't know if Cal knew that Jill was likely involved with her father.

"You're so stupid, Abby, you played right into us…." He parked the car in front of the office front of a small warehouse. "You should have stayed in New York for a while. Once you got back, all of this would have been over and you wouldn't be involved at all. To tell you the truth, I'm actually sorry it has to end like this."

I was terrified and confused at this point. Girls had died, Jill had lied to me, and now I had somehow gotten myself smack in the middle of some scam based on the premise that I wanted to help Darcy, who didn't even want to be helped in the first place.

"Cal, it doesn't have to be a disaster at all. Let me help you. I can connect you to someone I know very well in New York and maybe he can help set things straight or at least help you with a plan." I considered telling him that the FBI was already in place but didn't think it would help me at all, especially since I was concerned that Phil had lost us.

"Who do you know in New York?"

"My ex-boyfriend, Jason, he's a cop. He has a lot of connections who know how to get people out of things, if you know what I mean."

"Abby, I don't think you realize how deep this goes, do you?"

"Cal, I don't know why you'd be involved in anything like this. Why would you risk it all?" I tried to appeal to the goodness that I thought I saw in him, yet I did not want to sound desperate or to let him see my hands shake.

"It's complicated, Abby. I owed the Lejeunes so much. When I started getting more involved with Jill, things really started to escalate."

"You guys are still together, aren't you? I knew I sensed something between the two of you." I felt as if Cal was going to start opening up to me.

"There she is." He turned the car off. I looked over and Jill walked out of the front of the warehouse. "Come on, let's go." For a second he walked ahead and I thought he might have left the keys and I could take the car, but he reached back in and grabbed them.

"Does she have everything?" Jill said to Cal as we walked up to the building. Cal nodded. "Anyone follow you guys?"

"No and would you believe she gave Walt the slip after she was at the bank? Brilliant, just brilliant!" Cal laughed.

"Jill, where is Darcy?" I asked.

"Abby, can you take your little goodie-two-shoes self and shut the hell up for a minute?"

"Jill, I thought we were friends? What about your article you were writing?"

"Oh, I'm going to write something, but it's going to be a different story than the one you're thinking of. I'm going to make sure it's an award-winner. Why couldn't you just have stayed away, Abby? Don't you see you've gotten yourself into more than you could possibly handle? My dad has been running this operation perfectly for a long time. Then he decides to get a little cocky and involve someone like Darcy, who didn't need to be involved, and look what happens! We didn't think you'd be so overzealous in a loser of a case. Dad thought I could talk you down from it."

"What's this about, Jill? I really don't understand."

"We've been running things back and forth on container ships for a long time. Through Cal, we got the customs' guys in our pockets, so this has been running smoothly. Then we get an opportunity through Dad's colleague, Dick, for a humanitarian proposition of bringing some girls in to work, you know, help some girls out from Poland. Dick doesn't tell us the whole story and we probably should have foreseen that this was pure trafficking. These girls were taken from Belarus, smuggled to Poland, and then put on a ship to us. Dad has been working on some legislation with his firm regarding human trafficking laws, so I don't know why he'd agree to anything as crazy as this, but he did. We'd done it a few times, and it worked out fine. For that matter, we gave them a better life then they'd have in Poland or Belarus. But then Pollyanna comes along...."

"You can't have seriously believed that smuggling girls had any humanitarian value?"

"I don't think we should tell her any more, Jill," Cal said. "We need to make all of this disappear."

"Jill, I told Cal, you know you can trust me. I can call Jason. He has some connections, maybe he can help you guys. I don't need to tell anyone about this. Just let me talk to Darcy."

"Sorry, Abby, I can't let you do that." Jill walked back into the office.

"Where is Darcy? Where is she?" I yelled at Cal and grabbed him by the shirt. He pushed me down on the ground.

"Probably in Louis Armstrong Park, I'd imagine." Cal pulled me up by my shirt and forced me to walk into the building.

CHAPTER 25

I felt completely defeated walking into the office with Jill and Cal. I'd ditched Walt earlier, when probably I should have ditched Jill and then Cal. I was overwhelmed, first from Darcy's case getting so screwed up, then my dad dying and having to race back home, and now from the immediate shit storm I encountered coming back to New Orleans. I didn't want to believe that Jill could kill me. I started thinking about Darcy being dead in Louis Armstrong Park and I couldn't help pondering what they would do to me. Escape—I needed to escape. Where was Phil? It seemed everyone I attempted to trust had somehow let me down, except, of course, for Johnny, whom I had let down terribly.

"Stop daydreaming, go over to that file and see what you can find." Jill had turned into someone I didn't even recognize. She seemed preoccupied but nervous. I could tell by the way she kept on rubbing her hands together like she was cold.

"Jill, I don't know what I'm looking for so I don't know how I can freaking help you." I was pissed, and I wasn't going down without a fight. "Can't you guys let me go? Nobody knows I'm back from New York—I can go back. I'll help to get what you need and then get a plane today." If I could keep them talking to me, I might be able to keep myself safe at least until Phil came with what I hoped would be a brigade, but that was wishful thinking.

"Abby, you can't even comprehend what you've gotten involved with. Dad has been working to try and prove you could usurp some maritime regulations and all of this assures us that it can be done. It's too easy, don't you see?" Jill turned back to the files she was rifling through and started throwing some of it in a bag by her feet. I wondered why she didn't just torch the place and destroy all the evidence. What was I missing?

"Why did those girls have to be killed if this is merely a stupid exercise? I don't believe you, Jill! Was our friendship a farce? I trusted you, and I thought you trusted me. You know you can still trust me, don't you?" I looked around the office to see if there was a good spot that I could run to. I was concerned that Cal had a gun and about what he might be willing to do with it.

"Jill, you don't need to tell her everything." Cal was starting to sound as if his coolness was unraveling. If those two started to fight, maybe I could make a break for it.

"Doesn't matter anyhow...does it?" Jill looked at me with disdain.

"Maybe we could work this out. She has a point...she could go back to New York." I couldn't believe that Cal was making a play to help me. It gave me hope.

"You don't know her, Cal."

"You didn't tell me you wanted to hurt Abby." Cal's voice was starting to get louder.

"It's a little too late for that, isn't it? Let's do what we came here to do, Cal." Jill's tone concerned me. I was running out of time.

I didn't know what they thought they were going to do to me, but I didn't want to hang around to find out, no matter what Phil had assured me. My heart sank when I saw Walt move by the front door. Cal must have called him to tell him where we were. Walt had to be the one that put the girls in the park. He was the closest and knew the park. What could make him do something so heinous?

While Cal and Jill were continuing to bicker, I decided I had nothing to lose by trying to make a run for it. I hadn't taken more than two steps toward the back door when Phil burst through the front door.

"Everyone down on the ground!" Phil had his gun drawn. I dropped so hard on the concrete floor that I could feel the bruises forming on my knees.

"Phil, watch out for Walt! I saw him out back!" I looked up from the ground and started pushing myself back up and scanned for cover in case Walt rushed in.

"Walt's with us." Everything Phil said was without hesitation and with robotic confidence. Then, I saw Walt slip in the back door. Damn, I thought, if I had only stayed with Walt, he was the one I could've trusted.

"You did a pretty great job of giving me the slip, Abby. All I wanted to do is try and protect you from whatever was going down. Cal, I taught you better than this and you too, Jill. I should have known you two were in cahoots based on your history together. We've been investigating your father for a while now, but you two... you shouldn't have gotten involved." He shook his head. I could see that he still had fondness for them, but that wasn't going to be enough to help them through this.

"Is Maurice secured?" Phil asked Walt.

"Yeah, I had the boys downtown pick him up when I was over with Abby at the bank and she ran away from me." He smiled at me.

"Abby, Darcy is in the car out back. She looked fine, but I was getting ready to give Phil some backup. Why don't you go out and take care of her while we wrap things up in here?"

"You fucking bitch, you messed all of this up!" Jill stood up, stumbling. Phil had put the handcuffs on her.

"You are such a disappointment, Jill. It's hard to believe I thought of you as one of my best friends. I feel like an idiot for trusting you."

Phil and two other uniformed officers besides Walt were starting to crowd the small office. "You two are under arrest."

As I left, I saw them take Cal and Jill into an unmarked police car. I ran around back to find Darcy in the Cadillac belonging to Jill's dad. "Darcy, holy shit—are you okay? They told me you were dead!" Her hands were tied behind her back, and I worked to unravel her from her bind.

"I think they were going to kill us both. Jill couldn't do it, so she was waiting for Cal. I'm sorry I got you messed up in this, Abby. I had no idea any of this was going to happen."

"I don't think either of us could have predicted this," I said and sat down next to her in the back of the car.

"I should have told you the whole truth from the beginning, but I was scared. I know it isn't enough to just say it, but I'm sorry." I gave her a hug and felt her hug me back tightly.

"I'm sorry, too, Darcy. If I hadn't gotten so caught up, I might have seen things differently, so I'm sorry for that. Are you really related to Jill? Is that how you got involved in all of this?"

"What I told you about my parents is true. But, yes, my mom did have a relationship with Jill's dad. He tracked me down, but she never told me. I wasn't too keen on having a relationship, but he offered me a job. I was kind of floundering in school in St. Louis, so it seemed like an opportunity to get out of town and it was an easy transfer with my school and sorority. The job, well, I'd have this little backup plan with Maurice supporting me. My mom was not pleased at all and begged me not to go. She's not even talking to me right now because of it."

"Moms are hard to deal with. Trust me, it's not easy. She'll come around." I wanted to believe this too. Everyone wants that fantasy of your mom being your best friend, but it doesn't always work out like that, even though I still had hope.

"After what happened, maybe my mom was right about him

after all. I mean, when something sounds too good to be true, you know?" Darcy laughed a little, likely out of relief.

"Trust me, I've learned my lesson and probably more about trafficking and maritime law than I ever thought I'd know," I said as my heartrate started to come down.

"For once in my life, I feel as if I did the right thing, even though it seemed so crazy. I mean, most people look at me and don't take me too seriously, that was, until I met you. You gave me the confidence to come forward and speak up for myself. You listened to me, you respected me, even though I know I drove you a little crazy." She smiled when she said this and picked at the bottom of her too short skirt.

"I think your mom would be proud of you, Darcy. I can talk to her for you, if you want." She'd risked a lot by trying to do the right thing and go against her birth-father, which must have been confusing.

"Hey, you girls need a ride back to New Orleans?" Walt asked. He'd come around the back of the building.

"FBI, Walt? Why didn't you tell me?"

"Abby, Mr. Lejeune has been under surveillance for a long time now. I couldn't risk breaching that confidence even though I knew quickly where you stood on things. You being there actually made a light bulb go off and I realized how they were getting a lot of their information. My guess is that Jill had been tracking you for a while now. When it turned out you had left in the middle of the night and were with Cal, I didn't know which side you were on. Of course, Cal working with Jill came as a shock to me. I never would have called him had I known. It must have made things quite easy for them."

When he said this I winced, as if I'd been punched in the stomach. I felt like such an idiot, as well as completely naive and desperate, for not seeing through Jill and considering her one of my best friends. I wanted to believe that not all of it had been a farce.

"By ditching you, I totally jeopardized my safety, didn't I?"

"Thank God you had the good sense to call the FBI directly. I'd hoped that you'd confide in Doctor Mackinaw when he called, but he told me you didn't seem as forthright as when you'd spoken earlier. He assumed that you might have been compromised."

"Does Doctor Mackinaw know what's going on?"

"No, but I think you should give him a call back anyhow." Walt gave me a wink when he said this.

"What happens now, Walt?"

"Well, all the maritime issues are federal matters, so it's going to be a process. I'm sure you'll have to be involved. You're not planning on leaving town any time soon, are you?" He said this and helped us into the Cadillac.

"The car I drove over here is parked in the Walmart lot nearby, but I'm not sure how to get there."

"Abby and I are going to go to Thailand." I raised my eyebrows and looked at Darcy. She shrugged. It seemed like a crazy but good idea. After what we'd both been through it was a great idea to take a few weeks off and travel, go see Val and regroup. "All we need to do is buy tickets."

"I don't know if I can take any more drama. But you need to promise me that there will be no more secrets."

"For now, both of you better get your butts home and listen to the news. Sounds like there's a big storm brewing in the Gulf so don't get yourselves lost or anything. After the preliminary hearings, I think there'll be a little lag time before you are needed so you could go to Thailand then." Walt grinned at Darcy.

As we drove into the strip mall area, I pointed to Candice's bug out in the middle of the parking lot. "Feel embarrassed that you couldn't find me in this car?" I nudged Walt. He started to laugh, then Darcy got into a fit of giggles and I started laughing too, a welcome release from what we'd all gone through.

My phone rang and I tried to control my laughter, hoping it might be Doctor Mackinaw again. I was looking forward to telling him how things had turned out. "Abby here…" was what I could manage through my laughter. There was silence on the other end of the phone. "Hello? Hello?" I was about to hang up when I heard his voice. It sounded like he was right next door. Walt and Darcy were busy laughing at the sight of Candice's car and not paying attention to me.

"I'm at your apartment. Where are you?" His tone had a little bit of an edge to it.

I nearly stammered when I said, "Jason, what are you doing here?"

"I have to talk to you about Johnny."

I tried not to gasp when he said this because having Jason in New Orleans could only mean something was very wrong. My heart jumped up in my throat as I realized the relief I'd felt was only a reprieve for what was to come….

ACKNOWLEDGEMENTS

T his book took many twists and turns over a long period of time, culminating into my MFA thesis and then evolving, with many people to thank along the way.

To my esteemed professors at SUNY Stony Brook, especially Lou Ann Walker, Bob Reeves, Roger Rosenblatt, the late Frank McCourt, Billy Collins, Melissa Bank, Ursula Hegi, and Susan Merrill: your input was invaluable in helping me to craft my writing in ways that I never intended. I'm not the same writer as when I started, and for that I am grateful.

Writing partners are essential and Sande Boritz Berger has been both a dear friend and invaluable for all of my writings over the years. Reba Weiss provided some fresh eyes when I needed them most, and Fran McConnell did a powerful read when I could no longer see mistakes. Thanks to the many kind friends and readers who told me they loved it even when I knew it needed more work: Susan George, Wendy Lappenga, Jenese Beckstrom, John Krentel, Francesca Mercer, Carrie and Elsie Boskamp, Laura Crocker, Michael, Alexandra, Kate and Kristine McCourt, and others who read bits and encouraged me.

I'm grateful to the *East Hampton Star* for publishing chapters over the years. And to Debra Englander, with whom I connected quite serendipitously and helped me along the journey with Post Hill Press. To all at Post Hill who helped with the process with thanks.

And finally, to Michael and Lucy, who always support me with this "literature" thing I love to do.

ABOUT THE AUTHOR

ELIZABETH MCCOURT is a writer, certified executive coach, top-ranked financial recruiter, and professional speaker. She has also been published in a variety of genres in *Proteus, The Southampton Review, The East Hampton Star, On Wall Street, Mind Body Green, Huffington Post,* and *The Philosophy of Coaching: An International Journal.* More of her writing and www.mccourtleadership. com. She tweets at @ecmccourt.

Elizabeth has a BS in Finance from University of Maryland, JD from Loyola University in New Orleans, a Natural Resources Certificate from the University of New Mexico, and an MFA in Creative Writing from SUNY Stony Brook where she studied under a number of illustrious authors such as Frank McCourt, Melissa Bank, Billy Collins, Roger Rosenblatt, Ursula Hegi, and many others. Her coaching includes certifications from The Coaches Training Institute (CTI), the Hogan Leadership Assessment, and the Academy of Executive Coaching's Systemic Team Coaching method.

Her 2015 TEDx talk is titled, "Why You Should Spill Your Secrets." She speaks professionally about finding your inner warrior, fiercely female, resilience and leadership, and recruiting; in addition to moderating and participating in panel discussions on female-fueled leadership, writing and financial services recruiting.

She lives with her husband and dog, Lucy, in Westhampton Beach, NY, where they own Michael George Events.